Dedalus Europe
General Editor: Timothy Lane

TAKE SIX: SIX BALKAN WOMEN WRITERS

T0018172

TAKE SIX:
SIX BALKAN
WOMEN WRITERS

edited & translated by
Will Firth

and with the Slovenian texts translated by
Olivia Hellewell

Dedalus

This book has been selected to receive financial assistance from English PEN's "PEN translates" programme, supported by Arts Council England. English PEN exists to promote literature and our understanding of it, to uphold writers' freedoms around the world, to campaign against the persecution and imprisonment of writers for stating their views, and to promote the friendly co-operation of writers and the exchange of ideas.

Published in the UK by Dedalus Limited
24-26, St Judith's Lane, Sawtry, Cambs, PE28 5XE
info@dedalusbooks.com
www.dedalusbooks.comcom

ISBN printed book   978 1 915568 12 0
ISBN ebook   978 1 915568 38 0

Dedalus is distributed in the USA & Canada by SCB Distributors
15608 South New Century Drive, Gardena, CA 90248
info@scbdistributors.com   www.scbdistributors.com

Dedalus is distributed in Australia by Peribo Pty Ltd
58, Beaumont Road, Mount Kuring-gai, N.S.W. 2080
info@peribo.com.au   www.peribo.com.au

First published by Dedalus in 2023
Translations & editorial material copyright © Will Firth 2023 except for Slovenian translations which are copyright © Olivia Hellewell 2023
Texts which are in copyright are copyright their individual authors.

The right of Will Firth to be identified as the editor and Will Firth and Olivia Hellewell to be identified as the translators of this work has been asserted by them in accordance with the Copyright, Designs and Patents Act, 1988.
Printed & bound in the UK by Clays Elcograf S.p.A.
Typeset by Marie Lane
This book is sold subject to the condition that it shall not, by way of trade or otherwise, be lent, resold, hired out or otherwise circulated without the publisher's prior consent in any form of binding or cover other than that in which it is published and without a similar condition including this condition being imposed on the subsequent purchaser.

A C.I.P. listing for this book is available on request.

WILL FIRTH

Will Firth was born in Newcastle, Australia, in 1965. As a literary translator, he focuses on contemporary writing from the Serbo-Croatian speaking countries and North Macedonia. He graduated in German and Russian (with Serbo-Croatian as a minor) from the Australian National University in Canberra. He won a scholarship to read South Slavic studies at the University of Zagreb in 1988-89 and spent a further post-graduate year at the Pushkin Institute in Moscow in 1989-90.

Since 1990 he has been living in Germany, where he works as a freelance translator of literature and the humanities. He translates from Russian, Macedonian, and all variants of Serbo-Croatian. In 2005-08 he worked for the International Criminal Tribunal for the former Yugoslavia.

His translations include Aleksandar Gatalica's *The Great War*, Faruk Šehić's *Quiet Flows the Una* and Tatjana Gromača's *Divine Child*.

OLIVIA HELLEWELL

Olivia Hellewell was born in Sheffield in 1988. She translates contemporary fiction from Slovene and is Assistant Professor of Translation Studies at the University of Nottingham. She wrote her PhD thesis on the translation of contemporary Slovene fiction post-1991, and her recent translations have included Goran Vojnović's *The Fig Tree* and children's titles *Adam and his Tuba* and *Felix after the Rain*.

In 2020-21, she was Translator in Residence at the British Centre for Literary Translation.

CONTENTS

INTRODUCTION

This third book in Dedalus' *Take Six* series is devoted to contemporary women's prose from the Western Balkans, specifically from the six Slavophone countries that were part of Yugoslavia until the early 1990s: Bosnia-Herzegovina, Croatia, North Macedonia, Montenegro, Serbia and Slovenia. Beginning in the 6th century CE, much of the Balkan Peninsula was settled by Slavic tribes, who began assimilating and displacing older inhabitants. Throughout the Middle Ages, the northern and central Balkans were ruled by a flux of different Slavic principalities, with Byzantium and Venice seeking to make inroads from east and west respectively. Today's Slovenia and most of Croatia were long part of the Austro-Hungarian Empire, whereas other regions of former Yugoslavia have a history of Ottoman rule going back as far as the 14th century, when the Ottoman Empire gained decisive control of the region in the Battle of Kosovo (1389). Ottoman holdings in Europe began to decline in the 19th century, and Serbia — a suzerainty since 1830 — achieved full independence after the Russo-Turkish War (1877-78). Bosnia-Herzegovina came under Austro-Hungarian rule in 1878 and was formally annexed in 1908. Montenegro, where the dynasty of prince-bishop Petar II Petrović Njegoš had carved out a de facto independent principality within the Ottoman Empire, was recognised by the Great Powers in 1878. Ottoman power in the Balkans collapsed completely in the early 20th century, and the historical region of Macedonia was hotly contested. Its partition between Serbia, Greece and Bulgaria resulted in the First Balkan War (1912-13) and Second Balkan War (1913). The portion occupied by Serbia went on to become part of Yugoslavia after World War I.

The Kingdom of Serbs, Croats and Slovenes was formed in 1918 by the merging of diverse territories. Colloquially known as Yugoslavia (literally 'land of the south Slavs'), the state was officially renamed the Kingdom of Yugoslavia in 1929. During World War II, the country was invaded by the Axis powers in 1941, quickly conquered, and divided into several occupation zones and quisling entities. A multi-ethnic resistance movement formed, and under communist leadership, began to achieve significant military successes from 1943. With some British intelligence support and aid from the Soviet Red Army in the north, the Yugoslav Partisans were able to liberate the country largely by themselves by May 1945.

Parliamentary elections were held in November 1945, at which the communist-led National Front secured all the seats, and a government of the Communist Party of Yugoslavia was established in 1946. The long-term prime minister and later president for life was Josip Broz Tito. The Federal People's Republic of Yugoslavia was formed the same year. The country was ruled with the same Stalinist ruthlessness as other Eastern Bloc states. Following the Tito-Stalin Split of 1948 and Yugoslavia's expulsion from the Cominform, the country began to take an independent course in world politics, shunning the influence of both West and East. Estrangement from the Soviet Union was used to obtain US aid via the Marshall Plan, and Yugoslavia founded the Non-Aligned Movement, which it went on to play a leading role in. After reforms in 1953, Yugoslavia experimented with ideas of economic decentralisation and self-management, where workers had input into the policies of their factories and shared a portion of any surplus revenue. The Party's role in society shifted from holding a monopoly of power to being an ideological leader. In 1963, the country was renamed the Socialist Federal Republic of Yugoslavia. It became increasingly integrated into the world economy, with large Western companies investing in the country, raw materials being sold for the world market, large numbers of Yugoslav citizens working abroad (and often sending money back home). Western goods and popular music were available in Yugoslavia and its beaches and cities like Dubrovnik popular tourist destinations

A brief excursion into linguistics: Bosnian, Croatian, Montenegrin and Serbian are mutually intelligible variants of the polycentric South Slavic language formerly known as Serbo-Croat(ian) and today often referred to with the acronym BCMS; although separately codified, they are united by a single grammatical system and a largely overlapping vocabulary. Four of the authors in this book write in this language. Slovenian and Macedonian, on the other hand, are markedly different in grammar and word-stock. BCMS, Slovenian and Macedonian are interrelated to a similar extent as are English, Dutch and German.

Many specialists consider Yugoslav policy towards minority languages to have been exemplary. Although three quarters of the population spoke BCMS as a native tongue, no single language was official at federal level. A range of community languages enjoyed official status in the constituent republics and provinces, e.g. Italian in Croatia; Hungarian, Ruthenian, Slovak and Romanian in the northern Serbian province of Vojvodina; Albanian, Turkish and Romany in the southern province of Kosovo, etc. A total of sixteen languages were used by newspapers, radio and television stations, fourteen were languages of tuition in schools, and nine at universities. This was arguably a fair and progressive recognition of the country's linguistic diversity. The Yugoslav People's Army was the only institution of national significance that used BCMS as the sole language of command. However, this legal equality could not disguise the factual dominance of BCMS. As the language of almost 75% of the country's 22 million inhabitants, and of the centre of power in Belgrade, it functioned as an unofficial lingua franca. It was a compulsory subject in all schools, whereas significant smaller languages such as Slovenian, Macedonian and Albanian were not taught outside the respective region at all and their status was correspondingly low.

Tito's death in 1980 saw an increase in centrifugal forces within the federally structured country. Hyperinflation and fiscal debt exacerbated the political and economic crisis, with the relatively prosperous republics of Slovenia and Croatia in the northwest pushing for increasing independence, though it is fair to say that all the republics developed a certain intransigence, and Serbia in particular wanted to preserve Yugoslavia at all costs. The collapse of the Eastern Bloc in 1989-90 amounted to a death-knell for Yugoslavia, with neither East nor West any longer perceiving its need as a buffer. The consequences continue until today: de-industrialisation, structural maladjustment, corruption and a brain drain are ongoing problems. Not to mention the rampant nationalism that prevails in many places. Tourism on the Adriatic coast is an important source of income for Slovenia, Montenegro and especially Croatia (21% of GDP prior to the Corona pandemic).

It is hard to generalise about ex-Yugoslav literature, given the great diversity within south-eastern Europe. Latin and central European influences were strong, particularly in the part of the Balkans closer to Italy and the German-speaking region. Yet it would be fair to say that all these literatures — with the possible exception of Slovenian — bear at least a trace of Byzantine and Ottoman heritage. They are generally receptive to European and global trends thanks to a long tradition of translation, encompassing the Russian classics, Latin American magical realism (Borges, Márquez, etc.) and much more besides. Yugoslavia's early break with the Eastern Bloc meant that so-called socialist realism in the arts did not dominate for long: Miroslav Krleža, a leading Croatian intellectual, gave a speech at the Third Congress of the Writers' Union of Yugoslavia in 1952, which is considered a turning point in this regard. Yugoslav writer Ivo Andrić, best known for his novel *Bridge on the Drina*, won the Nobel Prize for Literature in 1961 'for the epic force with which he has traced themes and depicted human destinies drawn from the history of his country'. These literatures often reflect the experience of communism (sometimes humorously, like Slavenka Drakulić's *How We Survived Communism and Even Laughed*), reveal the existential challenges of system-change and migration, and — overtly or subtextually — manifest the rich geopolitical perspective of being located at a major crossroads. In a world dominated by a handful of great powers with their own orthodoxies and ways of seeing, 'minor' literatures can deliver fresh and exciting works that help us think outside the box.

Women's writing in the countries that were once part of Yugoslavia is certainly not a new phenomenon. Individual female writers have made their mark since the Middle Ages, such as the Orthodox nun Jefimija (1349-1405), the poet Anica Bošković from Dubrovnik (1714-1804) and the Croatian children's writer Ivana Brlić-Mažuranić (1874-1938). With the spread of compulsory education in the twentieth century and the socio-political aspirations of both upper-class women and the socialist movement, the number of female writers grew. Yet even today it is often a struggle for women to assert themselves as writers in a patriarchal society where writing is widely perceived as a male domain.

Three late 20th-century writers relatively well known outside the Balkans are Daša Drndić (*Trieste*; *Belladonna*), Dubravka Ugrešić (*The Museum of Unconditional Surrender*, etc.) and the abovementioned Slavenka Drakulić, all originally from Croatia. Few female writers from further south or east have enjoyed an international breakthrough, but mention should be made of Vesna Goldsworthy, who writes predominantly in English (*Inventing Ruritania, Monsieur Ka*, etc.), Jelena

Lengold (*Fairground Magician*), Marija Knežević (*Ekaterini*) and the poet Ana Ristović, all of them nominally Serbian.

It is probably correct to say that no female writers from the region of former Yugoslavia can make a living from creative writing alone — readerships are small and the creative sector is underfunded. The same applies for the vast majority of their male colleagues. Writers are aware of their position and can arguably allow themselves greater freedom than if they were pandering to the purported expectations of 'the market'; on the other hand, there are often other pressures, for example to conform to national norms and canons.

This book brings together a wealth of styles and themes and celebrates six remarkable Balkan women writers.

Note on the Pronunciation of Names

We have maintained the original spelling of proper nouns. Vowels are pronounced roughly as in Italian. The consonants are pronounced as follows:

c = ts, as in *bi*ts
č = ch
ć = similar to č, like the t in *fu*t*ure*
dž = g, as in **g**eneral
đ = similar to dž
j = y, as in **y***ellow*
r = trilled as in Scottish; sometimes used as a vowel, e.g. 'Krnjo,' roughly **K***ir*n*yo*
š = sh
ž = like the s in *plea*s*ure*

MAGDALENA BLAŽEVIĆ

BOSNIA-HERZEGOVINA

The seven short stories from Magdalena Blažević's acclaimed 2020 collection *Svetkovina* (Celebration) portray the lives of women in rural Bosnia in the 1980s. They focus on women's experiences in rigid patriarchal and religious communities, dealing in particular with sexuality, illegal abortion and infanticide — issues that women find it hard to talk about even today and that are insufficiently represented in literature from Bosnia-Herzegovina. The stories' combination of poetic terseness and stark imagery, often with elements of folk tales, is scintillating.

LULLABY

Baby Bunting, bye
Tanja mustn't cry.

The bicycle bounces along the country road. It winds and follows the railway track. In winter, the rails are grey ice. They screech beneath the iron blades. Tanja grips the metal handlebars of the bike. She is a dry stalk of corn that rustles in the north wind. Dew falls on her. It makes the bicycle rust, and Tanja decays. She stinks of barn. Of cow. She keeps a wooden stool by the wall of the barn, under the nail with the rope. She places the stool beneath the cow and sits. The cow swings its tail and slaps her in the face. Dry pieces of dung cling to its hairs. Tanja ties the tail to the cow's leg.

'Easy, Milava, easy!'

She strokes the cow's big belly. Both it and the udder are balloons inflated to bursting point. A hard female belly just before giving birth. Tanja washes the cow's teats with cold water. It moos loudly. She squeezes a spongy teat. It is a deflated penis. White glass bottles in the bicycle's basket. Tanja leaves them on the wooden doorsteps. Hay is stuffed between the bottles. Like hair. Tanja cuts hers short so it doesn't burn on the stove. It turns black and shrivels on the hot plate. The remains are invisible and disperse in coaly smoke. Her hands don't know what to hold on to. They clench up in the warm fabric of her dress. His words are slimy and hiss in the fire. When the grip on her head subsides, her hands are still frozen with fear. Like in a dark room. Fear of long arms from under the bed that could grab you by the legs. The heat singes her cheek. She'll make sure to turn the other one next time.

Night birds screech
They peck at the windows

At dusk, Dušan's car drives down to the riverbank. It emits coaly smoke. It and the dusk are the same hue. Nevena is lying on the back seat. She is covered with a blanket so no one will see her when they drive through the village. The darkness beneath the blanket stinks of stagnant river. The car stops between the treetops and the upright bushes. The river burst its banks in the autumn and inundated them. It receded to leave slimy waterweed in the bare branches. From afar, the treetops are made up of motionless black birds. Dušan spreads the blanket on the pebbles. It is as dusty as potatoes from the cellar. On the blanket, Nevena spreads her big white thighs. A black bird between them. Dušan pushes in a finger. It is slimy like the waterweed. He wipes it on his work trousers. Nevena's breasts are taut bovine udders. Pink-blue. Dušan sinks his teeth into them and licks them with his raspish tongue.

Nevena's belly rises and hardens. Her nipples stand up one way and another.

He's ever closer,
Can you hear his steps?

The flour is as dry as the dust on the potatoes. A snowy hill in the basin. Tanja shakes the sieve and puts it down on the board. Dry moths and their eggs in a silky net are left in the sieve. She crushes them between her fingers. She hears the door creak. She wipes her hands on her apron.

A little girl sleeps in a cot under the window. Her head is a healthy, round apple. Yellow-red. Shadows fall on the apple. As black and long as waterweed, as Dušan's coat hung up on a nail in the wall. Tanja grabs him by his sour finger. By his flaccid member. She pummels him on the chest.

'You've been whoring again!'

Dušan's hand is big. Tanja's whole head fits into it. He holds it over the hotplate of the stove. There is milk in a round pan. A thin, whitish skin forms on the surface. Tanja sees it out of the corner of her eye. When the fire dies down it will cool and stiffen. Like Tanja's cheek.

He knocks on the door
The floorboards creak

Tanja looks at her watch. She hears its loud ticking. She knows the train will soon stop. Through the window she recognises the low roofs and the willow grove by the river.

The little girl in Tanja's arms is a restive goat. She struggles and whines.

'Sh-sh-sh-sh-sh-sh-sh-sh…'

Tanja's mouth is a lullaby.

She waits for the murmur to subside and leaves the carriage last. She sits on a bench with the little girl and waits for darkness to fall. As thick as Dušan's blanket. So that curious eyes will not see her through the windows. She knows the way to her mother's house by heart. Along the railway track and then towards the field. The windows of the house are yellow and cast shadows on the cornfield. It was harvested with a sickle. The stumps are black from the damp. Stalks stacked high. In the dark they are big thorns.

Tanja knocks on the door.

He's right behind you
Can you feel his breath?

Before dawn, her mother's house is mute and cold. The stove is as icy as the rails. Long shadows creep into the room through the window. Black, silent birds. Tanja sits on the edge of the bed. Her feet are bare. Her long arms stretch towards them. She covers the little girl.

The door hinges creak. Tanja is light and transparent. Frost beneath her feet. Dense clouds in her mouth.

Grey ice on her neck. The iron blade passes easily through her putrid flesh.

The grey ice screeches.

Baby Bunting, bye
Tanja mustn't cry.

THE MILL

The child was not christened, so the grave was dug beneath an ancient yew behind the cemetery fence. Neva stands over it, as skinny as an old hen. She holds Tonka by the arm, whose head is covered in a black scarf. Her eyes, two blurry spots on a pockmarked face, stare blankly. Her body rocks feverishly. Neva's wizened hands try to calm her.

Neva takes a crumpled handkerchief from her sleeve and gives it to Tonka. She opens it and wipes the mucus from under her scabby nose.

The rope scrapes the bottom of the coffin. It smells of fir. A squeeze on Tonka's arm. At Neva's sign, Tonka bends and scoops up a clump of dry earth. First there is a dull thud, then a crumbling on the lid of the coffin. Dust under her nails.

Children's heads in a row behind the fence. Mute eyes follow the small gathering.

The shovel is thrust into the loose heap with a harsh sound. The gravedigger, hunchbacked Kekez, covers the coffin with swift swings of his shovel. Soil and drops of sweat are in the air.

The cross is a pointed stake knocked together from an old board. A deeply notched wooden block stands in front of

Kekez's house. The grass is covered with splinters and chips. He drives the cross into the top of the mound with three blows of the axe butt. Thudding. Tonka covers her ears with her hands. The carved letters are shallow and crooked.

Neva takes a candle from her pocket. The wick glows. She sticks it in Tonka's hands. The grave has no flowers. Only a single bluish flame flickers on it.

The mourners, all women, disperse with a hushed murmur. They wave to shoo home the children. Their skinny legs scatter.

Neva and Tonka leave the cemetery still arm in arm. Kekez remains behind. He smokes, leaning against the fence. He watches their covered heads as they go. They disappear behind the blossoming hedge. He crushes the cigarette butt with his dirty boot and clears his throat.

His shovel is slung over his hunched back. The wooden gate creaks.

An old, mudbrick house. Its foundations have sunken slightly and the walls are cracked. Blackened cross-beams hold them in place. A gentle slope above the house. Rowan trees are in bloom. Their crowns abuzz with bees. Rotting scraps of food lie scattered in the grass in front of the door. Two yellow cats are pulling them apart.

The lock of Tonka's door is broken. The door is tied to a nail in the wooden frame. Neva undoes it. The door bangs against the wall.

Down from the house is a road. A cloud of dust and a blue police car. A sturdy officer, cap in hand.

'Comrade Tonka Budim?'

Heads turn.

Screams erupt from Tonka's mouth. Her lungs without air.

'What is it?' Neva's voice is calm. Her hands hold Tonka's trembling body.

'I have a few questions, Comrade!'

Neva leaves Tonka and goes up to him.

'Don't ask us anything. You can see she's crazy — she doesn't know anything.'

'She's crazy, she doesn't know anything,' Tonka repeats.

'The baby was stillborn. I saw it with my own eyes,' Neva says, lowering her voice.

Tonka howls.

The police officer glances at one and then the other. He puts his cap back on and returns to the car without a word.

The room resounds to Tonka's screams. Neva helps her lie down on the wooden bed under the window. She takes off Tonka's shoes and unties her scarf. The room is cold, without light. Curtains on the window.

Tonka's hair is braided into a black wreath. Lustrous. The prematurely aged face beneath it seems even more miserable. A woollen rug over her trembling body.

'I'll be back later,' Neva tells her.

'I'll be back later,' Tonka repeats and closes her eyes.

Tonka is hiding in the attic. She sits on the wooden floorboards. Her legs spread, bent at the knees. She rocks from side to side and cracks her knuckles. Before her is a huge, almost pointed protrusion. Her waistless dress is filled by a belly and heavy breasts. Terrified by the pain, she locked the door, climbed the wooden stairs and drew back the bolt on the hatch to the attic.

The roof window is dirty. Faint light falls on a thick layer of dust.

Unbearable pain. Hot waves sweep over her. She wipes away the sweat.

The pain stops briefly. She is overwhelmed by sleep and weakness. Her head leans against the wall.

Every new stab is stronger. Sharper. Her hands are beneath her belly. She groans loudly and evenly.

Water drips from her stockings. She removes them in panic and squats.

She props her hands on the floorboards. Her mouth is dry. Silent. Her body convulses against her will. Her womb expels blood and a tiny, skinny body. Tonka observes it wide-eyed. She feels the umbilical cord and jerks at it madly. Ichor splashes from her womb again with remnants of tissue. There are cracks between the planks beneath Tonka. Blood leaks through them.

The tiny body is motionless. She lifts it up and studies it closely. It waves its little arms and legs. Loud crying.

Tonka throws it to the floor and covers her ears with her hands. The baby falls silent for a moment, then screams even louder.

Tonka's knees scrape across the floor. Thick swirls of dust rise from it. She opens a wooden chest. Out with the dusty blankets and coats. She takes the baby by the legs and throws it into the chest. She covers it with woollen layers. The crying dies down. She closes the chest and latches it. Silence.

Neva knocks at the locked door. She is holding a pot of soup.

'Tonka! Tonka! Open up!'

Neva puts the pot down at the door. She walks around the

house and peeks through the window but sees nothing. She goes down to the road and looks both ways. Not a soul in sight.

She hurries up the hillside beneath the rowan trees. She goes along the forest path. Shade and birdcalls. Cats have gathered at the door. They ravenously devour Tonka's meal.

Neva brings hunchbacked Kekez. An axe gleams in his hand. He shakes the doorknob hard. He motions for Neva to stand back, swings and smashes the lock. The door opens. Pieces of wood and rusty metal on the floor.

Neva can't see Tonka.

'Tonka!' she shouts.

Kekez stays at the door.

A drop of blood falls from the ceiling onto Neva's arm and runs between her prominent veins. Neva looks up. She races up the stairs and thumps the wooden hatch. It rattles loudly.

'Open up, Tonka!'

Tonka groans on the attic floor. At the sound of Neva's voice, she lifts herself up, crawls to the hatch and pulls back the bolt. She sees Neva's torso in the opening. Tonka kneels in her bloody dress. Neva climbs in and feels her flaccid, deflated belly.

'What have you done, wretched Tonka?' What have you done?'

She looks around. She kneels in front of Tonka, grabs her by the shoulders and shakes her.

Tonka points to the chest. Woollen rags land on the dust and blood. At the bottom is a tiny lifeless body.

She crosses herself and wails.

Kekez's head in the opening. In front of him, Neva mourns over the chest. Tonka rocks to and fro on the floor, her head bent.

Large drops of sweat collect at the bottom of his chin and slowly fall to the rough wooden floor.

Tonka's key on the doorpost. She looks neither left nor right at the level crossing. She walks along the hedge and is lost in the cornfield. The leaves are thin and sharp. Shallow cuts on her face and arms. Dry, cracked earth beneath her. Columns of ants emerge from the cracks. The loud flutter of a jay.

A wheatfield separates Tonka from the willow grove. She leaves a flattened trail behind her. In the bushes, a hare stretches on its hind legs.

Tonka among the willows and alders. The hedge is dense. It obstructs her view. Thorns cling to her dress like clothespegs. The River Bosna murmurs. A zephyr of freshness.

The mill is a hut with a shingle roof. It sits on rough-hewn logs atop a weir. Its door is wide open.

The waterwheel clatters. Unsightly Krnjo emerges from the darkness. When he was a baby, his mother once left him in a wooden playpen in the middle of the kitchen. The door was left ajar, and hungry chickens flocked around him. They pecked his bare legs. Unearthly cries resounded through the house. Alarmed by the boy's screams, the chickens jumped at his face. They pecked away the fleshy part of his nose. All the way to the bone. He wasn't taken to the doctor. They applied ointment and bandaged the wound. It healed into a curved stump.

He shakes the flour off his coat and looks around. He whistles briefly once.

At his signal, Tonka rushes to the mill. They disappear

into the dark interior. Tonka giggles loudly. He puts a finger to his lips. Tonka repeats by putting a finger to her own.

Powdery dust and bran fall into the flour chest. Tiny particles waft into the air. Trout gather chaff and flour dust under the waterwheel.

Tonka lies down on heavy sacks of corn. Krnjo's short fingers lift her dress. It is bunched up under her neck. The stench of urine. White lice flee from the seams of her dress and over her shaggy legs. They crawl over swollen scratch marks.

Tonka's eyes are rivetted on the roof matted with cobwebs. An empty hornet's nest.

Krnjo's hands rest on Tonka's breasts. His palms cover the large pink areolas.

His gaunt body is between Tonka's thighs. His horribly grimacing face looms over hers. Tonka closes her eyes.

Krnjo's groans and Tonka's incessant moaning are drowned out by the noise of the mill and the gurgle of the river.

Hunchbacked Kekez stands beneath the yew. Its branches are red with berries. He looks at Tonka among the old women in a black coat, bareheaded. She did not know where Neva put her headscarf. The wardrobe in the room was left open. Crumpled rags fell out.

The day before, she woke up in an icy room. The window pane was frozen in sharp crystal shapes. Neva had not come. She put on her slippers, and in her nightgown, made her way through the deep snow to Neva's door. It was unlocked.

She found Neva motionless at the low table, her head on the wooden board. A faint trickle of blood from her nose. Her hands still in a basin of dough. Tonka shook her and she fell to the floor. Out in the yard, she howled and hit herself on the head. The neighbours held her by the arms and legs until she fainted from exhaustion.

She stands over the grave. A black, open wound on the white hill with people crowded around it. She rocks from side to side and cracks her knuckles.

A mallet strikes the top of the cross. Tonka covers her ears.

Yellow candles protrude from the grave. A wreath of conifer.

Tonka goes down the road alone. Uncertain steps. Rowdy brats run in front of her and shout:

'Baby-killer, baby-killer!'

'She's crazy, she doesn't know anything,' she repeats quietly.

Night is falling over the village. Tonka leaves the steep road.

Followed by the shadow of hunchbacked Kekez.

POMEGRANATE

In the hallway under the stairs lives a wolf. It comes out at first dark when the lights are just going on. Although a lightbulb hangs from a cord, there's no light in the hallway, so I whoosh through it with my eyes shut tight. That way, the wolf can't hurt me. The fire in the stove has gone out. The empty grey in the window has cooled and silenced the house. They've left me at home alone. This time they took my sister. Usually they leave her for me to mind. She holds onto the hem of my trousers and follows me wherever I go. She's scared of everything. In the winter, a Gypsy woman in colourful pantaloons knocked on our door. Her coat was black. I let her into the house to see how scared my sister was and how old and ugly the Gypsy was. She stank. She dropped her bag to the floor. It was big and empty. She stood by the stove and warmed her hands. My sister hid behind the wardrobe. Curled up in the corner like a cat. She would have fitted in that bag. Night was falling, as it is now. The Gypsy didn't say anything. She pulled the door shut behind her. I looked out of the kitchen window at the path, but she was gone. I'm sure she was eaten by the wolf in the dark under the stairs. I should have told her to shut her eyes.

In the hallway, my heart pounds in my ears. When I open my eyes out on the verandah, I see yellow spots. My gumboots are wet, but I put them on all the same. The first autumn rain has fallen, cold and fine. It's made deep, dirty puddles on the path, so I run past Grandma's garden. Mud clings to the soles. The glass on the door of Grandma's larder shed shows yellow. They must be in there. Next to the house is a plum orchard. The trees are black and upright like Grandpa. Only brandy can fell him. It cuts like a chainsaw. Then Grandpa crawls and growls. He pounds on the wooden door of the outhouse with a pole. Grandma cries there in the dark. When she comes out, purple plums stand out on her skin.

Grandpa doesn't plant anything else, so I eat plums all year round as soon as the blossom falls from the branches and the tiny fruit embryos can be seen. They crunch under my teeth. Their pits are soft. They taste like young grass. I eat until Grandma sees and my tummy starts to hurt. She's afraid nothing will be left on the branches. There's no fruit around our house. The meadow is full of dandelions. Mother uses the leaves for salad. They're as bitter as green plums. When the plums ripen, Grandma uses them to make a pie. They turn the dough purple like her skin. In the backyard, Grandma stirs jam with a pole. Flies whirr around her head. They get in her eyes like with a cow grazing. Grandpa doesn't mess with jam. He prepares big vats for brandy.

'When you get married, make sure your husband isn't a boozer.'

Grandma freezes the excess plums. She takes them out

in the winter when there's nothing else sweet. The defrosted plums smell of the freezer and stagnant water. I eat them like the green ones. Until my tummy hurts.

A jumble of shoes in front of the larder shed. Among the muddy peasant footwear and galoshes are a pair of dainty red leather boots with high heels. No woman in the village wears ones like that. Mother wears nice shoes to work, but they're all black. I think these are just right for my feet. Small and narrow. I try them on. Now I'm tall and beautiful. I take them off again and open the larder shed. It's dark and warm inside. The ceiling is low and only one lightbulb hangs from it. No one notices me. They talk loudly and smoke. Uncle is visiting from Slovenia and has brought his lady friend so the family can meet her. She's as dark as a Gypsy, but young and lovely. A suitcase stands by the door, and on it a hat with a ribbon. Half a pomegranate lies on the edge of the table. My mouth waters. It's heavy in my hand. I crawl under the table. Her name is Natalija and she'll be having a baby in the spring. They won't get married until the baby is born. Grandma feels it's not right and wipes away tears with her scarf, while Grandpa drinks toast after toast. The bottle is already empty. The red seeds are juicy and sweet. My mouth is sugary. Images from Grandma's bible come to mind. The birds and flowers in paradise are as wonderful as the pomegranate. That's why I think there's a God. Once, in church, my father lifted me up onto his shoulders and away from people's smelly coats. What a ceiling, and statues with flowers! And chandeliers of cut glass like in the palaces in my picture book. I'll show them to Grandma because she just stares at her hands in church. This isn't the first time I've eaten pomegranate. It was a year ago. I was coming back from school alone. I was wearing a dress for the first time. My tights were itching and kept falling down when I played elastics in the break. Grandma wouldn't like to see me lifting my legs in a skirt. Only strumpets lift their legs like that. The red seeds lay scattered along the road. Someone had gone that way before me and eaten pomegranate. In the sun, the seeds looked like capsules of fish oil. I take two every morning. The doctor says I'm malnourished. Mother feeds me all the time and it makes me feel sick. She fears the doctor will tell the whole village she doesn't cook for us. I ate all the seeds along the way. They didn't make my tummy hurt.

Our house is made of concrete. Only the ground floor is furbished, so dust keeps falling on us from the first floor. Pigeons coo under the roof. Mother sends me and my sister to bed as soon as it gets dark. We drink goat's milk for our bronchitis and then go to bed. The milk makes my tummy hurt more than the plums. Mother turns off the light and closes the door. Then the wolf comes out from under the stairs and growls. I hear it scraping at the door. My sister and I cry in the dark. We don't call Mother because she doesn't like that. My sister falls asleep before me. I hear Mother and Father when they go to bed. They whisper. He climbs on top of her, she kicks and struggles. I pretend to be asleep, but she always knows when I'm awake. The milk makes me want to pee, but I don't get up. In the morning, Mother strips off the bedlinen and washes the mattresses. She yells at us. I'm less afraid of her than I am of the wolf.

The rain has stopped, but the sky still hangs grey and low. I stand in the middle of a puddle. Like my sister in the Gypsy's bag. I slap the water with a stick. I disappear. Everyone's in the backyard except Grandpa. He hasn't sobered up for days.

When I get married, my husband won't be a boozer.

The morning wind cuts to the bone. Mother didn't cover herself, so she curled up next to father. Natalija is wearing a short skirt and nylon stockings. She must be cold too. I wonder if Grandma thinks she's a strumpet. Uncle carries the suitcase and shakes hands. She kisses us, holding the hat with the ribbon. When I grow up, I'll get on the train and leave this place. I'll wear red boots and a hat. I'll go where the pomegranate grows.

THE WALNUT TREE

Day breaks, and Anika, wife of Vukašin, has not yet closed her eyes. She stands at the window, as motionless as an owl. The blue light strikes the coarse features of her face. Dark round eyes and a hooked nose. Her lips swollen with lust.

She stares at the black stump. The walnut tree used to shade the house, rustle and tap at the window. Then, last summer, it burned with a terrible flame. The fire crackled and blazed. The leaves curled up into charcoal aphids. The tree burned down to a black eyesore. The wind blew hard and carried the smoke and charcoal aphids through the village. They fell on the roofs and gardens, and got into people's mouths. The villagers inhaled that grey mist until it rained. The rain washed them out in sooty drops. They poured down cheeks and windows. Old Bogoje chopped down what remained of the tree. The blows of his axe were sharp and crisp like a tooth biting a piece of charcoal. Although the tree is gone, its infinitely long veins still run beneath the foundations of the house. Anika still feels the shadow of its branches. Its leaves still rattle in her head.

Anika's black hair is full of damp dawn and the haze that has risen above the cornfield. The stems are dry and thin. Broken in places. The ground between the rows of corn is trampled, with marks of rubber soles. Anika squatted in the pitch-darkness, her bare legs bent. Like a toad over a red bilge. The damp earth clung to her shoes and got under her fingernails. It stained the heavy cloth at the hem of her dress. Night birds shrieked over her as she ran down the paddock. A warm bundle in her arms.

Anika's arms and cheeks have fine cuts. The burrs of the tall burdock are hard and sharp. Their tops are clenched fists. They grow in a ring around a deep hole between the paddock and the potholed road.

In the village, they call that hole the Bomb.

There, between the paddock and the village road, the air flashed during the great war. The earth trembled to a deafening roar, and two scrawny cows were flung sky-high. They were blown to smithereens like the windows of the houses. Pieces of carcass lay scattered around the deep crater. The bowels of the earth opened up, as dark as well water.

Loud croaking at the bottom of the Bomb. The sacs on the frogs' throats bulge almost to bursting. A baby lies face down in the shallow, stagnant water. Its mouth and nose full of mud. The greenish-black water runs into its ears and behind its neck. Its skinny hindquarters are peeled frogs' legs.

Anika takes off her loose dress.

The rough bark of well-hidden orchard trees is imprinted on her back. Andrijaš leans her against them when night falls. He has white, manicured fingers. He slides them under Anika's skirt. Between her spread thighs. His fingers are then as slimy as Anika's protruding tongue. On Sundays, Andrijaš puts a flaky piece of altar bread on it. When it sticks to Anika's palate, she soaks it with saliva, compacts it with her tongue and swallows it.

Her breasts are swollen and heavy. Infinitely long blue veins have branched under the skin. Andrijaš buries his pointy face between them. An insatiable shrew. His voice is a lecherous murmur and his tiny eyes close.

Her nipples have darkened. They are wrinkled like two wormy walnuts.

In the village, they say Anika is barren.

She puts her dress and scarf away at the bottom of the wooden chest. Her nightgown is long and loose. Strips of rag between her legs. She lies down next to Vukašin. His wooden crutches lie on the floor. His breathing is gravelly. It rends the air, and Anika hears the bursting of the walnut tree's bark and the crackling of the fire. Bark beetles pour from his half-open mouth and fill the room. They bump against the windows and Anika's eyes.

A well-fed, ginger tomcat emerged from the cornfield. The hard green stems swayed briefly. It snorted loudly in front of Anika's door, then scooted up into the walnut tree and started caterwauling like mad. Torn-off leaves, dry pieces of bark and a rain of split walnuts fell from the tree as if during a summer storm. A blood-curdling yowl rent the torrid air and abruptly interrupted people's afternoon naps. A knife fell from Anika's hands to the wooden kitchen floor. Stunted potatoes in a bowl of water. Their thin, dusty peels in a trough. Vukašin got up from the bed. One of his trouser legs was empty. It swayed like an empty sack. Anika moved aside the curtain of the ground-floor window and saw the tips of the branches tapping at the window like long thin fingers and the walnuts in split husks rolling down the drought-stricken paddock. Her face was a shroud. Cold and pale. She crossed herself and went fearfully out of the house. Vukašin remained at the door on his crutches.

Anika threw stones up into the walnut tree. Fear-stricken faces gathered in front of the house. Their throats were dry. The cat raged even more fiercely, and they imagined it could leap down and devour them at any moment. They shrank back.

A blinding flash of lightning split the serene sky. It struck the tree and instantly set it ablaze. Zigzagging cracks appeared in the parched earth and deepened. The flames roared as if from an open furnace. No buckets of water from the well could put it out. The whole tree was consumed. The villagers stood helplessly, their eyes fixed on the sky.

'The devil's got his due!' Vukašin shouted from the door. 'Foul things are afoot!'

'Shut your gob, old fiend!'

Anika threw a stone at him.

Thick black smoke billowed above the tree and danced seductively in the clearing of heaven.

The road beneath the paddock is full of puddles. A fine layer of crystal clings to the edges. It crumbles under Bogoje's gumboots. A sharp-pronged pitchfork over his shoulder. Eyes in the shade of a wide-brimmed hat. A long-haired black-and-brown mongrel runs ahead of him. Its ears flap up and down.

The Bomb is an open grave. It gives off a repulsive stench. Rotten meat and pondweed. Hoarfrost is on the burdock. The dazzling white has turned them to icy decorations. The dog's muzzle peeks through the stalks first. It snarls and shows its sharp teeth. Bogoje knocks down the burdock with his pitchfork. Frost rains from their tops. The dog barks. It springs at the pitchfork. Bogoje kicks the dog. It yelps.

The frogs are gone. There is only the small body at the bottom. As black as Anika's belly under the corset of bandages. The skin beneath them is wrinkled and split. Sinuous earthworms on putrid soil. Bogoje kneels down and lifts the baby with his pitchfork. Its body is on sharp prongs like an overcooked piece of meat on a fork. The impression of the body remains in the hole like in a plaster mould.

A crowd gathers around Bogoje. They fold their hands and raise their eyes to the heavens. Anika runs down the paddock. Her dead breasts bounce beneath her dress. Beneath them is flabby, furrowed dough. Her fingers dig into the heavy cloth. Vukašin stands below the house, leaning on his crutches. He yells after Anika and raises a crutch high into the air. His trouser leg swings. Beneath it the stump of a leg. Misshapen like the burnt remnant of the tree.

Horror is etched on Anika's face. Her lips are parted. Pale. Without a word, she goes down to the road and hurries to Andrijaš's door.

She knocks with a trembling hand.

She begs for his blessing.

WILLOW

The school hallways are empty old pipes. The air smells of cellar and darkness. Of rotten floorboards and mice. The walls are daubed to shoulder height with an oil-based paint that was once green. Above it, greying whitewash. The school doors closed long ago and silenced the murmur. The semi-darkness beneath the stairs is paradise. Late spring rustles through the ragged plastic sheeting on the windows. It casts quivering rays and shadows of the tall pines on our bare skin. I don't close my eyes. I want to remember everything. The faint light diluting the darkness, Marko's dry lips and hot breath. Our panting is loud and resonates in the empty space. I let him lean on me. His weight is captivating. He unbuttons my trousers and puts in his hand. It's colder than my skin. Silky. Bees buzz in my ears. Honey flows in my mouth.

'I'll strip you naked one day, you'll see.'

That makes my belly fill with stones. My throat runs out of air. It smells of brambles from the field and wild roses. He pulls out his wet, shiny fingers and smells them.

Sharp teeth on my tongue.

A warm wind blows through the holes in my tights. It announces evening.

41

Willow, let your sap run free
Though it be the death of thee

I mutter a prayer and bash a willow branch with a stick. I score it with a knife. The thin bark slides off easily. A slippery snakeskin. The stripped stem is a crooked white bone. It makes my fingers wet and shiny. I climb high into the upper branches and blow the whistle. The sound spreads out over the roofs. From the treetop, the village is different. Strange and distant. I'm untouchable here.

The rain has turned the stream's gurgle into a roar. Mother told me to tear off three willow sticks this time. They mustn't be too thin. They're supple and tough like the leather whips for cattle. However hard you hit, they won't break. I go up to my mother's room first. It always smells the same. Of worn dresses and morning breath. I leave the sticks in front of the mirror on the wooden dressing table. Now I can count six of them. I pull down my trousers and wait. I hear banging pots and splashing tap water downstairs.

Then silence.

Mother's steps are sharp and heavy on the stairs. She closes the doors and windows firmly. So that no one will hear us. In the mirror, my legs are crooked white bones. Mother says she'll damn well put some colour into them. To drive the devil out of me. Father then leaves the house. He walks down the road and smokes. The first blow hurts the most. It makes the skin go numb. I don't cry. So Mother hits harder. The bruises are invisible at first but very soon turn the colour of fresh black pudding. I bend down and rub them. The willow cane is a razor. It cuts my cheek and shuts my eye.

Mother drops the canes. She grabs me by the hair and turns me towards the window, then runs downstairs to the bathroom. A jet of water. It's warm in her room, but my teeth chatter. My body shakes. Mother presses a wet towel against my face. That makes it hurt more. I lie on the bed and Mother covers me. The bedcover is as icy as the stream below the willow. Rain runs over my face from the towel.

Mother closes the door behind her. As she leaves, her footsteps are inaudible.

The bruise on my face is the colour of overripe sloes. I hide it with my hair. The head of my aunt's baby is the same colour. Mother says it was strangled by the umbilical cord while still in her belly. They named it Elena. The coffin is small. It lies open on the kitchen table. The baby is tiny even though they say it was big at birth. The two silk ribbons of the bonnet come together under the chin and seem to strangle it.

The door to my aunt's room is open. She lies on the bed covered to her belly. It protrudes like it did before the birth. Her cheeks and eyes bulge like a frog's. Mother helps her express the milk. She squeezes the breasts and thick milk spurts from the big black teats. Like from a sprinkler in the garden. Mother wipes it up with a towel.

My aunt doesn't go to the funeral. She won't get up for forty days. Mother says the birth was difficult and they barely managed to get the baby out. There are long meandering stitches between her legs. As black as my bruises.

Father and uncle are in front of the house, waiting and smoking.

On summer evenings, no one can find me. I'm not even up in the willow. It's as empty as the dried-up stream. Mother calls for me in vain. Even when she falls silent, her voice rings in my ear. I run into the field. I disappear behind a hedge of white hawthorn. The darkness there is paradise, like beneath the school stairs. I lie in the grass. It's as dark and delicate as forest moss. As Marko's eyes.

'I told you I'd strip you naked one day,' he says in my ear.

That gives me goosepimples. My skin is translucent dandelion. I unbutton myself. Red primroses have sprouted on my chest. They grow in Marko's mouth.

Mute darkness descends quickly and quietly in the field. It makes the air cold and damp. The lights of the village don't reach this far. Marko's eyes, too, have disappeared in the darkness. I feel his grip on my arms and the heat of his body. I don't even recognise his voice. It's distorted. A locomotive roars over me. The grass is sharp now and presses into my back. It tears the skin. I grit my teeth.

I sit high up in the willow. My legs are streaked the colour of fresh black pudding. My belly has swelled. Burgeoned.

I'll wrap the cord around the baby's neck.

I climb to the top of the tree. Where the branches are thin and young. So that the crash will be harder.

> *Willow, let your sap run free*
> *Though it be the death of thee.*

BROODY

Below Vrančug Hill is a dense, dark forest. A goshawk descends over it, swooping low. It cries loudly above the house of Zagorka Boroz. For a moment it disappears among the low, grey clouds and emerges again, wings extended. Its eyes diffuse from yellow to red. It circles over the backyard and then plunges at the henhouse. The raptor's screeches drown out the cackling and the flapping of wings. Downy feathers waft through the fence to land in a muddy puddle.

The wind blows in gusts, harder and harder. It bends the branches of the apple tree and they beat against the windowpanes overgrown with ivy. The thin glass shakes. Zagorka takes a metal basin from the cupboard and glances at the windows. The wooden stairs beneath the eaves creak beneath her feet. She is wearing black, with thick stockings beneath her dress and her head in a scarf. She goes out into the muddy yard bounded by a fence of thin birch sticks like bones. Her black gumboots sink into the sodden earth.

A tall black mulberry tree stands with branches outstretched over the henhouse. The overripe fruit lie scattered on its roof and on the ground. The acrid smell of decay mingles with the odour of chicken manure. At Zagorka's squelching, the disturbed chickens scurry towards her.

'Shoo, shoo, shoo!' she waves her long arms.

In the henhouse Zagorka finds the half-plucked, bloody body. The neck is bare, the throat torn out. The basin falls from her hands. She raises her eyes to the sky and wails. And curses aloud. The frightened chickens cackle. She grabs the muddied, dead bird by one leg and throws it onto the rubbish heap behind the shed. The smell of blood attracts the crows. They croak loudly.

She picks up the dirty basin with trembling hands. A pounding in her chest. Her head and torso vanish in the opening of the henhouse. The broody red hen has a nest in the corner. It takes pieces of straw in its beak and throws them over its back. Zagorka puts some straw in the basin, slides her fingers under the hen, and it ruffles its feathers. Its tail fans out like a peacock's. Its head turns quickly, its fleshy comb shakes. Zagorka gently lifts the bird and gathers up the eggs. One by one she lays them in the basin.

'My Reddie, my sweetie,' she soothes it with her bony fingers.

Thin purple skin under Zagorka's lead-grey eyes. Cobwebby wrinkles have taken hold at the sides. Dark blue strands of hair protrude from her scarf. They mellow the severity of the black scarf. She takes the hen with both hands. She feels the warm, silky feathers and slender bones. She places it under her right arm and takes the bowl of eggs in her left hand.

Katuša stands in front of the henhouse, her arms crossed under her large breasts. The wind lifts her dress. Her knees are swollen, white. Her veins blue and knotted.

'What are you doing with the hen, wretched woman? Don't make her hatch those eggs, if you've an ounce of goodness in you!'

'Mind your own business, old hag!'

Katuša comes closer and a stifling heat radiates from her corpulent body, together with pungent odours.

'He's only just been buried. His grave is not yet cold. You give him no peace in the other world either. The devil take you!'

Zagorka's face twists into a grimace. She purses her lips. Her eyes flash.

'What are you doing here?'

'Listen to me! The inspector called by this morning. He asked where Vidak was when they found your Nikola under the railway track. I don't know how you bewitched him, but from now on you'll leave my son alone. Since you've started meddling he neither eats nor sleeps. He won't be coming to see you any more, you can be sure of that... you barren shrew!' Katuša hisses.

She leaves without looking back.

The wind roars in Zagorka's ears. Her throat tightens as she restrains her tears.

A clap of thunder.

Katuša hurries down the slimy path and disappears among the black poplars in the field.

The cellar door is ajar. Cold air flows in. Dim light enters through a small, dirty window. The semi-darkness reveals wooden boxes with sprouted, rotting potatoes under blackened hessian sacks. Damp and decay. Tools, wreaths of onions and bunches of dried flowers hang upside down from hooks in the wall. Zagorka puts the egg bowl and the hen down on the floor. Next to the door is an old beehive with hay. She puts it up on the old wooden table and loosens up the hay. Then she places the eggs in the middle and sets the hen on them. It builds a nest, using its beak to shift the eggs underneath it. Zagorka speaks to it softly. She shuts the little door of the beehive, locks the cellar and puts the key in her pocket.

The day is waning. The sky has darkened and descended over Zagorka's roof, devouring the chimney. A few large raindrops fall on her face. They roll down her chin. She takes off the cover of the well. A silent prayer on her lips. Her face goes dark on the swaying surface of the water. A cold updraft. Muted echoes. Water splashes several times. She pours it into buckets. As she goes up and into the house, water from the brimful buckets spills over the stairs and the colourful woven rugs.

Only one window is lit up, illuminated by two burning lamps. They give off black smoke. Holding two tea cloths, Zagorka takes a pot of hot water off the stove. She pours it into a tub. She cools it. Thick drops of basil[1] oil drip from a vial. They spread on the surface of the water and form large shimmering patches.

A clap of thunder. Raindrops drum on the roof. Water flows down the drainpipes. Zagorka's fingers undo her headscarf. It slips silently to the floor. Her sheeny hair is tied back tightly in a bun. A few sweaty strands cling to her neck. The wind

---

1 Basil has religious significance in many Balkan countries, e.g. sprigs are placed on graves, hung up in memory of someone who has died and used to prepare holy water. In this story, together with Zagorka's black headscarf, it helps indicate she's a widow.

whistles through the decrepit window frames. The long, black fingers of the apple tree tap harder and harder.

The metal buckle of her belt clinks. Tiny buttons are pulled from their holes. The dress slides from Zagorka's spindly body. She lets down her stockings to reveal delicate skin covered with light-coloured hairs. She pulls the silky white petticoat over her head. Her breasts are firm and slightly apart, her hips rounded. Thick, golden fleece beneath her navel. She lets her hair down and slides under water. Her body curls up like in the womb. She closes her eyes. The long strands drift briefly in all directions, as lively as a brood of vipers, until they gradually darken and sink beneath the water.

It is dawn of the twentieth day since the broody red hen has been sitting on the eggs. The shell of the first egg breaks. First a yolky yellow wing emerges, waving helplessly, and then the rest of the unfledged, wet body. Cracks appear on several of the other eggs at the same time.

Just enough light enters the room through the window to transform all things into black spectres. They are motionless, cast on the walls. Zagorka sleeps wrapped in a featherbed. She is a caterpillar. Only her face protrudes from the cocoon. Under the bed, a long-legged spider spins its silky threads. It crochets slowly, flawlessly. All that can be heard is the soft scratching of a mouse in the wooden floor.

With the sun, the shadows recede silently into the wall. The spider settles in the centre of the web. Loud cooing comes from the gutter. Zagorka opens her eyes. They are bright and vivid. Clearly outlined lips gently parted. Her face is pale.

Her warm body slowly emerges from its shell. First her arms, then her legs. They spread on the spacious bed. She bends her knees and lifts her nightdress. The fingers between her legs are wet. Her body writhes and spasms with pleasure. Two serious, olive-tinged faces regard her from the headboard. A wedding photo retouched beyond recognition. Zagorka closes her eyes to it.

Her feet are bare on the wooden floor. The door hinges creak. She goes out onto the porch. The cool makes her bristle like a cat. The windows of the houses are open. Headscarved women in the backyards. Their hands scatter corn. The yards crow and cackle. Stifled mooing from closed stalls. Zagorka looks down the path towards the tall black poplars. Her eyebrows arch. Hot tears run down her face. Her body shakes with bitter weeping. She wipes away the tears with the hem of her nightdress, goes back inside and slams the door. She punches the wall. A wail of desperation rings through the house. She throws herself on the bed and buries her face in the white pillow. She soaks it with tears and saliva as she smothers her sobs. Then she gets up and wipes away the tears. She opens the sideboard cupboard and takes out vials of fragrant oils and balms. The glass rings. She washes herself with a decoction made from oak. The yellowish-brown liquid runs from the bush of her crotch. She dries herself with a hard white cloth. It softens on her wet skin. She rubs in the essences. She combs her long hair and ties it firmly in a knot. It shines golden. She takes a clean dress out of the wardrobe and puts it on, taking care of every crease. Tightening the belt, she stands in front of the mirror and sighs deeply.

Zagorka is light-footed. A silent ghost gliding down the path overgrown with white hawthorn and tiny wild roses. The rain and wind have scattered their petals. The sun is rising. Strong light falls on her face to show fine yellowish freckles. Her hair is aglow. It glistens. In her eyes the tall poplars pierce the sky. They refresh her soul. She hears the chirping of the birds and dry twigs breaking underfoot. She's closer now. Her abdominal muscles tighten and her womb feels heavy.

The field is bathed in sunlight. Several of the previous year's haystacks are still standing. Tall grass with wildflowers in bloom. Beyond it is Katuša's house. A low, red-roofed bungalow. Multicoloured daisies and asters grow along the fence. The yard is empty. Zagorka sits down behind a haystack and just peers from time to time at the house and the windows. Her eyes darken.

The last chick of Reddie's clutch hatches. A soft cheep in the dark of the cellar.

Zagorka sits behind the stack with her legs outstretched, her back against the fragrant hay. Insects come out of the grass and crawl up her legs. They swarm all over her dress. She takes an apple and a few walnuts out of her pocket. She crushes the walnuts in her hand. Her fingers run over her palm. She eats the brownish-yellow kernels. Sweet apple juice squirts under her teeth. She peers tirelessly at Katuša's house. Fine dust falls from the hay onto her face and sticks to the drops of sweat.

The door of Katuša's house opens and slams again. Zagorka jumps up.

She peeks from behind the haystack and sees Vidak in

the yard. His shirt is unbuttoned. His skin tanned, his fair hair tousled. Zagorka's body trembles, her legs would run to him by themselves. Her voice wants to shout. It echoes in her head. She hides behind the haystack and waits. She listens and hears the sharpening of a scythe.

At the sound of footsteps, hot and cold waves rush over her body.

'Vidak! Vidak!' she calls under her breath.

The scythe is flung into the grass.

Vidak's eyes are aglow. He hugs her and leans her against the haystack. Zagorka cannot make out his words, her ears are abuzz. He lifts her dress and spreads her moist thighs.

'Do you know how long it's been? You never came…'

'I couldn't. They don't take their eyes off me. The police came, too.'

'I'll be waiting for you tonight!' she says in his ear.

She slips out of his arms and disappears into the deep shade. She runs, beaming.

Vidak stands in the field and watches her go. He rubs his face.

Midnight. The broody red hen pecks the first chick to death. Red on fluffy yellow.

At the same moment, the stairs creak beneath Vidak.

Zagorka listens. Her hair is down. Her body naked. Its outlines can be glimpsed in the darkness. Silk fabric slides beneath Vidak's fingers. It evades his touch. Zagorka takes his hand. Familiar smells in his nostrils. He closes his eyes. She shoves him onto the bed and straddles him. The bed creaks under their weight. Zagorka's nails dig into Vidak's shoulders. The room echoes with their hot panting.

The red hen pecks the last chick to death.

The room is sunny. The branches of the old apple tree hang still. Zagorka lies naked. She runs her fingers over the sheet, now cool. An impression in the pillow. She dresses and combs her hair. The water on her face is cold. She looks from the verandah towards the black poplars. She smiles. She goes down to the cellar and unlocks. A flapping and a screeching in the beehive. She undoes the catch on its little door, and the red hen lunges at Zagorka.

At her shining, lead-grey eyes.

DRESSES

The floral wallpaper is wrinkled. Irregular yellow blotches. The room is a damp matchbox. The iron bed leans against the wall, below the curtainless window. The pane is cold and dewy. Ringed outside by rambler roses. Not a single flower, just thorns. The air is stifled by the cold darkness and a blue dust that spreads in Nataša's nighttime exhalations and morning strokes of the comb. Opposite the bed, by the door, is an open wooden wardrobe and an old dressing table with a mirror. Lacquered oak. Tired dresses on the coat hangers. Silk stockings shaped by Nataša's reed-long thighs, small knees and narrow feet slung over the wardrobe door.

She wakes before dawn. Watery gloom in her eyes. Heavy and dispirited. Only on rare sunny days do two yellow irises grow out of them. Then the orange-red capillaries sparkle. She gets up and steps barefoot on the tattered lambskin. The reflection in the mirror is a blurry silhouette. Nataša closes her eyes before it. She turns on the flickering light, puts on her slippers and pulls a dressing gown over her nightie. The narrow hall in silence. The doors of the rooms are closed. Her steps are sluggish.

Darkness in the open bathroom window. Nataša makes

out a wet, harvested field, black birds, broken bushes and a grove of alders. The stream gurgles from forest rains. She closes the window and undresses. The jet of water over the bathtub is an icy spring. Her dressing gown and nightie lie on the tiles. The hairs on her spindly body stand up. White, frothy skin like milk straight from the udder. She wets the flannel. Quick watery drops run down her back and between her round breasts. Her nipples stiffen. Ripe bog bilberries. The blue dust has crept between the hairs under her armpits and in the luxuriant black bush below her navel. It collects on the wet cloth. Red marks on her skin.

Her silk stockings are cobwebby. Unforgiving of dry skin and hangnails. She bunches them up before pulling them on. They are laddered on the toes and thighs. She takes a needle and white thread out of a biscuit tin. She lifts her leg onto the chair in front of the mirror. The needle creeps through the thin fabric. An uneven trail behind it. She mends the holes on the thighs with red nail polish.

The belt on her dress is tightened. Her waist is white morning glory. She washes her dresses in a basin with a piece of softened soap and hangs them up under the eaves in the yard. They dry quickly in the summer, they are hot and rustle, but in the autumn you can't get the damp out of them. She brings them in before dark and hangs them over the stove in the kitchen. They hiss in white smoke like lidded cooking pots.

Nataša in front of the mirror. She moistens the dry black cotton bud with saliva and coats her eyelashes. They curl up into wires. Sooty lumps fall onto her cheeks. She paints her lips red, puts her hair up and fastens it with a clasp. She leaves the house at dawn, her coat buttoned up to her chin. A jumble of muddy shoes at the door. The path to the road is all in puddles. It winds until it meets the asphalt. Now her heels tap. The morning damp creeps into her hair and softens the black coating on her lashes.

People wait for the bus in front of the village café. Glowing tips of cigarettes dot the air. The murmur dies down at the sound of Nataša's steps. Sidelong glances and sneers. Whispers behind her back.

The crowded, rickety bus stops with a puff. The door opens. Nataša squeezes into the crowded aisle. Rheumy eyes and greasy collars around her. Clamour full of morning breath. The bus lurches wearily over the rutted apron. A wave rolls through the sardined passengers and sucks Nataša under like a current. Only her delicate hand protrudes, gripping the high handrail. Her eyes in someone's back. She doesn't see the images of unfinished houses and hot chimneys flitting by in the window.

They get off at the same place every morning. In front of the primary school. The walls have windows. Painted half-way up in dull white. Tall pines around a stone bust in the yard, as ungainly as lanky children who've grown too fast. The passengers scatter in various directions. Nataša turns right, into the street that leads to the workwear factory. The shops on the left are closed. Bars on the windows. A line of withered trees on the right.

The factory is surrounded by a tall iron fence painted red. The narrow gate is open. A caretaker oversees the entrance. A monobrow and a moustache yellow from tobacco. He smiles and Nataša responds with a gentle nod.

The metal lockers in the hallway take up the entire wall,

like the windows of the school. The locks click, the doors bang. Clattering heels and loud laughter. Nataša's locker contains a green coat, workshoes, large dressmaking scissors and cotton wool.

'Good morning, Nataša!' Lina hugs her tightly and kisses her on the cheek. A trace of lipstick.

'Good morning!' Nataša laughs.

'Any word from him?'

'Still nothing. No letter, no postcard,' she says softly.

Lina pulls her by the arm into the queue for coffee.

They drink it steaming hot. They smoke fast and don't speak.

Nataša and Lina are at the sewing machines.

The hooter sounds for the start of the shift. 6am.

The sewing machines chug and whine in the big hall under the fluorescent lights. Hundreds of hounds chasing their quarry. Bent women's backs in workcoats. Their necks are bare. A cart with piles of blue twill arrives from the cutting section. The piles are shifted to the side tables. They spread a blue fluff that enters their mouths, nostrils and ears. It gets into their clothes and hair. Under their nails. It falls on Nataša's cheeks together with the black lumps.

At the hooter for a five-minute break, the noise of the machines subsides. A colony of green ants. A smoke curtain in the cafeteria. The large, trembling ceiling lights are crematoriums for moths. They incinerate with a sizzle. Lina strikes a match. Cigarettes stick to moist, round lips. Lina waves out the splint. Bluish smoke. A smell of sulphur. Nataša's gaze wanders. She turns around nervously.

Miloš comes up from behind and affectionately takes hold of her arm. Her senses give in to the scent of cologne. Black cardamom and pepper. A familiar, whispering voice buzzes in her ears.

He slips a piece of paper into her coat pocket and disappears. Nataša sticks her hand into her pocket and clenches the piece of paper. She laughs.

'What will you do when he leaves?' Lina asks.

Nataša says nothing. The light in her eyes goes out for a moment. She takes a last drag.

The covered sewing machines are black tombstones in the semi-darkness. The lockers in the hallway stand wide open. Mirrors on the inside. Nataša's face glows. She wipes it with a handkerchief. She adjusts her hair and paints her lips. The lines of her face are elegant. Full lips, a straight and rather long nose. Her coat sways on the hanger.

Lina is waiting at the illuminated gate. She hops up and down impatiently.

They walk arm in arm. The wind fresh in their faces.

Darkness in front of the entrance to Lina's building. Only the nameplate is lit up.

'Call and say I'm sleeping at your place.'

'What if your mum wants to speak to you?'

'I don't know, make up something.'

Nataša hugs her.

'I'll tell you everything in the morning.'

Lina stands in the dark and watches Nataša go out under the streetlights with her hands in her pockets.

She hurries along Osman Đikić Street, which leads to the Balkan Hotel. The city's cafés are half empty, the windows and their translucent curtains yellow. Cold sweat on the palms of her hands. Her heart pounds in her throat.

Miloš stands in the car park in front of the hotel, smoking under a linden tree. Nataša recognises him from afar. She sighs audibly. He sees her and throws away his cigarette. Crushes it. He rushes to meet her with outstretched arms. Nataša slips into his unbuttoned coat. As she hugs him, she breathes in the smell of the skin under the collar of his shirt. His hands on her waist. He kisses her hair. The scent of ripe quince. The stars in the sky are sharp.

The lock of Room 124 clicks open. Warm darkness and silence. Long, wet kisses.

Miloš turns on the weak light. Nataša's bag is cast aside.

'How long I've waited for you, my dear.'

Coats over the back of the armchair, one over the other. The silk threads of her stockings crackle beneath his fingers. Nataša lifts her dress and takes them off. A crumpled snakeslough on the carpet.

A woollen blanket flies through the air. The white bedclothes rustle.

Nataša unbuttons her dress. She whisks the thin negligee over her head.

A muscle on his face quivers.

Her bra and panties on the floor. The clasp clicks and her hair falls to her shoulders. Velvet amaranth.

A rising storm in Miloš's charcoal eyes. His nostrils flare. He comes up and lifts her hair.

'My beautiful Taša,' he murmurs, his eyes half closed.

His fingers work her delicate breasts. Delicate autumn crocuses.

The white sheet is stiff under her skin. Her thighs smooth as butter. They part in the glorious semi-darkness.

He breathes into her neck. He gently pulls her hair from behind. The aromas make him shut his eyes.

Loud cries in his ear.

The room is filled with pungent odours. Traces of blue on the crumpled sheets. Miloš is in a deep sleep. His body relaxed and sprawling. Nataša lies curled up beneath his arm. Her head on his bare chest. The pulse beneath his salty skin.

Her eyes are wide open.

Ž., 30.XI.1980
Sunday night

My darling,

I'm worried about you. It's been ten days since you left, and still there's no word from you. You promised to write every day. My heart is breaking and I don't know how much longer I can go on like this.

Lina is suspicious. She says I'm gullible, that you might not come back for me and that you have someone else there. I know you wouldn't cheat on me, would you? She doesn't know you like I do — that's why she says that. She doesn't know how good and gentle you are. I was relieved yesterday when she left to visit her family in P. I saw her off at the station, and now I miss her. I have no one to talk to.

I'm always alone, even when the house is full. I can't stand anyone and everything tires me. It's only eight o'clock, and I'm in bed already. I'm writing from under the covers because my room is cold. I couldn't stand sitting in the kitchen with the family any more. Mum keeps asking me because she's heard stories in the village. I don't want to talk to her about you because she wouldn't understand.

It's hardest when night falls. I shut myself in my room and turn on the radio. The music is wonderful. It calms me, but then I think about you even more. I close my eyes and you whisper in my ear. You kiss me tenderly like in our last night. I can hardly get up in the morning. At work, I talk only to Lina. Everywhere I look, I see only you. It's as if I'm just waiting for you to come up to me. I can smell your scent everywhere. I hear your voice. People talk to me, they laugh, but I don't hear a thing. I feel like crying and screaming so everyone will leave me alone.

The rains here are getting colder. Relentless and long. It stopped briefly in the afternoon, so I went out for a walk in the field. The ground is sodden and the trees have turned black. Only the birds and the flowering green hellebore by the road are alive. I wanted to go down to the river, but it was getting dark and there were lots of stray dogs.

It's pouring again. The rain beats against the window. I'll read from the book you gave me before I go to sleep. So much sadness in the title, We Two Will Part with a Smile. *We will be much happier. Just like you said — ours will be a land of milk and honey.*

My dear, I kiss and hug you. Please write back straightaway.

Yours,

Taša

The bus packed with workers from the second shift. They breathe the stifling darkness. The sound of the engine and the warmth stupefy their tired bodies. Nataša sits with her head against the glass and her eyes closed. She hears tiny, sharp raindrops striking the window. They turn into the first snow. Her senses drowse... naked skin and the rustling sheet beneath her fingers. His lips on her neck, his tongue tracing her veins. His fingers in her hair, their cries of pleasure. Incandescent bodies...

The bus stops with a shudder. Nataša raises her heavy eyelids. She holds on to the seat in front of her. The light in front of the café is in her bloodshot eyes and the star-like drops on the glass. The bus door opens and the cold air lashes her face. She hears her heels pound on the steps and splash in a deep puddle. Nataša's sleepy body shivers. The snowflakes are slivers of glass. They stab into her cheeks and hair. There is no footpath by the side of the road. Pebbles crunch under her soles.

Showers of rain and snow in the light bulb in front of the house. Nataša's hair is wet. Her coat has become heavy. Black drops on her cheeks. The north wind disperses them. The door is unlocked. Her mother comes out of her bedroom and turns on the light. Nataša puts her coat on the hanger.

'Your dinner's on the table. The postman came today and

had something for you.'

Nataša goes into the kitchen. A covered plate and an envelope are on the table. She recognises her own handwriting. The letter has come back. Address unknown.

She bursts into bitter tears.

'My Nataša… what did you think? That he'd take you with him? How many times do I keep telling you. They'll bad-mouth us now.'

Nataša says nothing. She slumps onto a chair and whines.

Her mother turns off the light in the hall and slams the door of her room.

The crumpled envelope in her hands. Her lips contorted with grief.

The light is off in Nataša's room. Her quiet sobbing is muffled by the bedcover. Tears and blue dust on her pillow.

Whiteness in the window at dawn. Light, dry snow and frozen thorns. Nataša's eyes are blank. The fine skin on her face is in red blotches. She gets up and leans on the windowsill. The grey sky has descended to the forest's conifers covered in white. The houses are in darkness. Only the occasional kitchen window is lit. Lazy smoke above the roofs.

Thin icicles hang from the eaves. Beneath them Nataša's forgotten dresses. Frozen. Immobile.

TATJANA GROMAČA

CROATIA

Tatjana Gromača's five pieces of travel prose are arranged chronologically to notionally follow the author's own path in life, from a provincial town in Croatia, where she was born in 1971, via the capital, Zagreb, to the Istrian peninsula, including a formative school trip to Kraków and a scholarship in Berlin. The texts' rambling, associative style touches on the many influences that have shaped the author's development and create a collage of today's Croatia in its Mediterranean and central European contexts. Gromača is painfully aware of the corset of expectations placed on women's writing in her country, should they venture beyond the 'permissible' genres of poetry and writing for children: 'Few women take up the challenge, and those who do, and manage to be successful, have often achieved this due to circumstances such as exile or emigration, beyond the confines of this society, through living and working in another culture.' She cites Irena Vrkljan (1930-2021) as a bold writer of this type, who introduced an air of the poetic and unconventional, the fragmentary and deeply subjective into ex-Yugoslav prose, accompanied by

an obsession with biographical detail. Virginia Woolf has also
been inspirational for Gromača.

THE CHURCH OF MARY MAGDALENE

The most beautiful baroque church in this continental part of Croatia. Built as an example of the perhaps somewhat unusual aspirations and designs of the baroque: to use the elliptical and domed forms of buildings to find a way to people's hearts, to open them for what religions, along with other endeavours, have been striving to impart for centuries — pliancy, meekness, understanding, or, as Confucius taught, reciprocity, *shu* — though with little or no success, and usually with quite opposite, catastrophic effects.

The builders of this church near Sisak are unknown. We know only that they were master builders from Italy, who used the labour of the local serfs — peasants from this sleepy, chilly region with its slightly swampy climate. Possibly due to scarce resources or needing to save, the builders also incorporated certain elements into the body of the church, material preserved from the time when Sisak was the Roman *Siscia*. Construction was completed and this beautiful church consecrated in 1765. A decade later, a Czech, about whom almost nothing is known today, except that he was Czech and named Joannes Franciscus Jenechek, built a particularly valuable organ in the church.

Where the fields of Turopolje merge imperceptibly into

the lowlands along the River Sava, with forests of willow, poplar, oak, hazel, beech and hornbeam, between the rivers Kupa, Odra and Sava, the unreal snow-white frontage of the church unexpectedly rises up with its uncommon, magnificent pair of bell towers, and then a person returning home from a journey can be very sure they've arrived.

The Church of Mary Magdalene, the most beautiful church in these parts, is unusual for its two bell towers and the elliptical dome behind them. The tops of the towers and the dome are made of anthracite-grey steel, almost black, in contrast to the white body of the church. It stands at the entry to a village, near a large livestock market. It's a delight to observe its fairytale towers and the dome merging with the sky in the background — be it a clear sky of delicate blue and cloudless, or obscured and cloudy, in harsh, sullen grey, or a sunny noon sky on a white, winter's day, when snow covers the ground, the surrounding graves and all the roofs except that of the Church of Mary Magdalene.

This church and everything around it is most beautiful on a clear, bright snowy winter day. When the winter twilight gradually descends over the village and this whole sombre region along the River Sava; when on the road with a thin crust of ice the returning traveller sees a tipsy man on a bicycle, in a fur hat, leather coat and gumboots, trundling along on a rusty bicycle like a strange contraption from a prehistoric amusement park, at risk of being swept away by a speeding vehicle; and when the returning traveller also sees that cyclist with a load tied to the rack at the back — a sack of potatoes or, better still, a gas canister or a slaughtered suckling pig — then it suddenly feels as if someone has put a key in their hands to unlock the secret mythology of this region, a kind of Vitebsk, a historical transition zone with its own remarkable backwood terms for everyday objects and concepts, and these have become the traveller's favourite words and give them a deep feeling of belonging to this obscure, dark ancestral homeland. And this region, with the man riding his bike in a winter night as a symbol, an archetype and bearer of life's essential and metaphysical meanings, doesn't end here; this signifier extends all the way along the River Sava, until it enters the Danube, where this image and this fateful scenery extends, to then go up along the rivers Bosut, Tisa, Begej, Brzava and Tamiš towards the Hungarian border and continue towards other plains in the Czech Republic, Hungary, Romania...

This returning traveller of ours, who is always equally dumbstruck and radiant when gazing at the two bell towers of the Church of Mary Magdalene, will definitely not agonise over the question of which century they've arrived in, which social and political system, since they *know* that here in this Vitebsk (certainly much less romantic than that of the Jewish-Russian painter Marc Chagall), in the region of the Church of Mary Magdalene, it would make no sense. Here Heraclitus' eternal recurrence of the same is forever in full force — the bowed people praying in the gilded church, with a rosary intertwined between their fingers, could be from this or that century, and the tax collectors who confiscate livestock or property for unpaid bills have only changed their hairstyles and attire.

An undefined sadness hangs over this whole region, over its poverty, subjection and cowardice, over the shame of those who've become rich through plunder and theft — probably the melancholy of existence. Only occasionally does a spark of *joie de vivre* glimmer. Everything here is left, in complete fatalism, to the will and actions of the gods, who never come or appear to finally take matters into their hands and see them through to a just conclusion.

This is why there's alcohol, born out of scarcity and despair at that emptiness; this is why there's that bike in the dead of night on the icy winter road with few streetlights, with only those two small pale-yellow lights. And this, ultimately, is why there's the Church of Mary Magdalene with its two towers like in Russian fairy tales, as if that which one does not live to see in this life, and has waited for so persistently and passively, will come when the soul, as light as a snowflake, soars up into the air, where the tips of these two bell towers are pointing, like an eternal prayer that never ceases.

ZAGREB

Zagreb is love at first sight, and also love from a great distance. That love always exists, even when you don't know the city, when it can only be seen from afar, or when you can sense its atmosphere and colour.

How do you get to know Zagreb, how do you learn to appreciate it and make it yours? It's best to love someone there, to move into a flat in New Zagreb together with them, and there — in love and warmth in those four small walls — to listen to music, live that youthfulness to the full, and watch the morning mists over the River Sava. The warmth and security of your other half's embrace is the most pleasant starting point from which to explore the city with its cafés and parks.

I say Črnomerec, and it's poetry to me; I say Trešnjevka, and it's poetry; Dubravica and Sesvete too; suburbs and outskirt towns with a ring to them. Zagreb is a symphony of a metropolis that never was, which has never had its broad avenues or triumphal arches, great palaces of justice or marble concert halls. It has always had only its grey buildings, the humble, sloping roofs of the upper town and its church precinct, Kaptol, with its soup kitchens and almshouses. It has its downtown Gajeva Street, with its funeral parlours and short, pudgy prostitutes. It has its trams, its surly, disgruntled people, its waggish service staff who greet customers with a casual *''ullo, love'*.

Zagreb is autumn, roasted chestnuts and mulled wine without cloves and cinnamon. It is bustling Kvaternikov Square on Maksimirska Road, with its closed-down shops that once sold knitwear by the metre, where there were shoemakers, watchmakers, leatherworkers and tailors. Zagreb meant craftsmanship and markets full of quality goods.

Zagreb is the highrise suburb of Voltino, but it's also small houses next to the River Sava embankment, enclosed by wooden fences, partly overgrown with brambles and tiny wild roses.

Zagreb, with its beautiful aristocratic houses, with a self-effacing elegance that hides poverty and abandonment, that veils the unfortunate fate of the decimated middle class with all its feeble trophies and successes.

Zagreb, with its salons, soirées, dresses and outfits, with its scales of values, with silent suffering and sighing for what there is not and what is unattainable. With envy and frustrations, which can sometimes be overcome.

Zagreb, with its flowering thoroughfares just opposite the central station. With pretty female students in knee-high boots who step with poise and aplomb, like well-trained parade horses.

Zagreb is a microcosm of everything Croatian, an amalgam of everything that simmers and seethes in that peripheral, humdrum history, which the rest of the world perceives as just a burden and waste of time. It is the accumulated whey of all the milk that Croatian children have imbibed in the provinces, which they've left forever, with the desire to bolster and promote the names of the families they stem from. Zagreb is a space imbued with the ambitions of those who were born there, those who came to it, and all their ancestors.

Zagreb is a walk through leafy Tuškanac and the Mirogoj Cemetery, and a trip to Mount Sljeme that abuts the city. It is a visit to nearby Japetić, Samobor, Podsused and Zaprešić. Zagreb feels so Croatian, but its speech — *lepo*, *belo* — can sound so Serbian. It is the uptightness of Croatia's parvenues and the wealth of its lawyers and advocates, architects and doctors. Zagreb is the norm and the rule for all; it evaluates and judges everything by its own standards, whose enthronement is achieved and consummated in ways sometimes dubious and less than sincere.

Zagreb is a simmering pot of civic roles, publicly shaped opinions and views; sometimes it is soundness, seriousness and authenticity; it is traces and remnants of old schools only glimpsed hazily today, and which, like Zagreb itself — loved unconditionally by so many and always universally recognisable — are at risk of extinction.

KRAKÓW

Oh, how would it be to roam those streets again that I roamed thirty years ago? But now, when I want to remember that city, I can hardly recall anything... hardly anything except a few places, earthly points of reference — some red brick, which could have been this or that, a big granary built to be dignified like a church, an arcade, in fact, wide and long like those that captivated Walter Benjamin in Paris, or like the one in Istanbul with the bazaar (and that dried saffron was so expensive). Yes, I remember that now, and it was in Poland, in Kraków! Several pairs of handmade leather slippers, elegantly rustic; a dark-red wooden box, inlaid with jade; an amber ring, a token inappropriate for my age (I'd just turned eighteen, and my role model was Virginia Woolf, who wore a similar ring). That's how much I've dug up so far, and there was more: old Wawel Castle, the tall cathedral, the famous university that great names passed through, but obviously I had no sense back then, only a dash of madness and courage, and quiet inclinations that worked away inside me, beyond my control, beyond everything actually... still, a playful side crept up and broke away from me despite the external factors, although there was also something benevolent in those external factors, as if they sought and found me, sometimes a little angrily, other times with a smile and a nod; all in all, something was taking shape, albeit uncertainly and with a lot of hitches (I'm the one who mostly contributed to that).

Now I'm settled and comfortable, so to speak, and I think back to times when it wasn't like that with nostalgia. Was it sensible to strive, to move forward to where I am now? The niche in life one has found can feel like a deep rut, like living boredom compared to what was before — an impetuous charge from one thing to another, a culture vulture drawn to everything: exhibitions, catalogues, monographs, music, painters, writers, photographers, philosophers, mystics, revolutionaries, artists of various kinds, performers, opera singers (yes, even them!), conductors, actors... you name it. What was I doing there anyway? Wasting time, as usual? Wasn't it a school trip? Only ostensibly; in reality it was more an anarchic journey. But yes, lest there be any misconceptions, communism still reigned in Poland, and how! Empty shelves in the shops, cheerless, monotonous food. Waitresses like ours, in blue skirts and white blouses, and punks like ours, drunk and convinced their country was the pits (ours shouted, hungover and overtired: *'Yugoslavia's the pits!'*). Yes, we were still Yugoslavia back then, that odious and deleterious construct, but for the Poles we were mega hipsters. Vodka from duty free shops, Camel Blue cigarettes, money spent like it was going out of fashion, with a feeling of material superiority; for a brief time there, we, the poor of the Balkans, had a chance to be spoiled dandies, and Polish poverty provided an exotic framework for our dreamy, post-pubescent delirium. Or was it just my raging fantasy carried to extremes by hormonal storms, for which a mere glance at Poland's quiet, peaceful and harmonious landscape sufficed to imagine mass shootings in those meadows and fields, in those pastoral and self-effacing forests: executions of various kinds, bodies falling into pits, graves that people had been made to dig for themselves before they were shot, in mute absence, without hope?

Indeed, wherever I looked for the whole duration of that journey, in the enigmatic, utterly silent landscape, which could seem sinister for a moment, I'd see just that: people expelled, dragged out of cattle wagons in their coats, frightened children, women with headscarves, men and old people, I'd vividly hear the ragged, raucous voices of soldiers, with bayonets fixed and their rifles pointed at the chests of that mass of people, shouting '*Schnell, schnell!*' And the people hurried straight to their deaths.

Afterwards I could see a time when everything turned back into a peaceful and inoffensive landscape, in the post-war period; and I could see a Polish farmer, like an abruptly awakened predator, set off into the forest in search of gold: gold teeth, a ring, anything of gold that remained of the executed Jews, who now lay under the ground in the loose forest soil yet to be excavated, and whose secret resting places it took the instinct of an unerring hunter to find.

And so dandyish banter, an anarchic pastorale crowned with cheap vodka (which our proletarian pocket could afford amply, unlike the Poles' in those days of the Iron Curtain) morphed into a moralistic discourse, and how could it be otherwise: we were in Catholic Poland, where people fall to their knees as soon as they catch a whiff of a cathedral, where they are reminded of their imperfection, with their hands mechanically folded level with their lips, which murmur monotonous, *zaum*-like words of prayer to Him — He, who looked on and perhaps concocted all of this, perhaps just so as to have a bit of fun, to while away the time.

I say this without bitter sarcasm, taking this thought at face value, as a plain fact, one of many possible equations, hypothetical of course, and as a tentative and speculative demonstration of human-divine perversion, where there is much blood, spilled entrails and severed limbs, which leaves behind a heap of bandages and gauze, sheets and rags, all filthy with encrusted blood, pus and human excrement; it all ends up in the seething cauldron of human history, the history of our civilisation (we're proud of it, after all), the one that built the Jagiellonian University in 1376, the second in Europe, on whose facade I long ago fixed my curious, innocent, tomboyish gaze; I guess it wanted to reach the faces and minds of those who'd taught there, those who performed the sacred duty of instruction, support and mentorship in the development of thought that should not be constrained, that should not flinch before the difficult paths of searching for truths that will probably never be found, but that does not believe in a goal and finality *per se*, that sees its goal and sense precisely in that search (which should be a kind of gold rush, but not for the gold buried with the bodies of those sadly executed in the Polish forests).

Therefore I strained my senses as I observed the facade of that great European university, which of course the Church was founder and patron of, in my attempt to conjure up those faces with the wave of a magic wand — the faces of its staff, past and present. But all that appeared were very restrained portraits of detached, pale people, who, to be sure, with almost fanatically glazed eyes and gazes, brought forth all manner of facts and figures, churned out quotes like broken old hurdy-gurdies, and didn't hesitate to laugh occasionally with a dose of petty malice and suppressed anger after making a comment that was supposed to be taken as critical, as independent-minded distance that was meant to provoke their audience, the students, to think.

Yes, but what did I actually want to say? How lovely it was back then? How proud that youthfulness was, how revolutionary, melancholic and maudlin as it stared into its future, and how touching it must have been to observe it in its good-naturedness, ignorance and idiocy? Everything it touched took absolute precedence for the simple reason that it was youthfulness, which seeks nothing *per se*, nothing but 'everything'; from this, through a process of 'deduction' known only to itself, youthfulness extracts a quantum of experience and knowledge for each individual bearer of that attribute, which, over the years and a series of transformations, is supposed to turn into so-called maturity, which is just a proud, conceited term that serves to conceal resignation and fatigue, illness and defeat.

That's why I can no longer remember Kraków today. I only know, I'm sure, that it was beautiful and young, brimming with churches, castles and palaces, but its suburbs were grey, monumental, mind-numbing and devoid of aesthetics, as befits communist buildings. In this sense, I prefer the church with its obvious, Gothic taste (especially in Kraków), which raises everything earthly to a non-existent dimension, but in a way pleasing to the eye and spirit, which I may not have been able to fully enjoy, and which, in contrast to the deaths and executions, the human disappearances that the sinister Polish forests preserve memory of, seemed like a humdrum trinket for middle-aged aesthetes and tubby art lovers.

It's hard to withstand the heartrending beauty of those mighty walls, squares and edifices, to resist the inclination to read meaning into those buildings, or at least their facades, when meaning as such at the same time loses all its weight, all its significance, if your gaze shifts from Kraków's old town towards that forest and the railway tracks that still run through it, and take you in a little over an hour to the infamous *Arbeit macht frei* sign.

Yes, maybe that's why we should go to Kraków and should see all that beauty and buoyancy, culture and piety, all that tradition: so as to perhaps better, more easily understand evil and hell. Or do they remain incomprehensible to us if detached from us, if they're not a product of our own inner monstrosity adeptly concealed from ourselves and the world?

But what did I know back then? Nothing at all, but I probably had a premonition because that evil preoccupied me to such an extent that I took possession of it. Not literally, of course, but I assumed care of it; it was a reflection that was meant to lead somewhere, to some primal principle that would make evil *per se* less painful, less cardinal and fatal in our consciousness and cognition, which could perhaps neutralise a degree of its seriousness and fickle theatricality. I ultimately wanted evil to lose the race, to be honest, and for the flag of goodness and truth, peace and freedom to fly throughout the world — or rather in every individual human life — and I will reinforce my incorruptible naivety and admit that I still want that today.

It's ridiculous but true: it was necessary to travel to Kraków back then and remember it today in order to admit it to oneself and face the shocking truth that failure is a necessary by-product of living on an axis of veracity and peacemaking that does sometimes arise and sparkle as a shining example, a model to follow, but only if we're advocates of unreality, of utopian, self-denying fanaticism.

Otherwise, in the vast majority of cases, such a life leads to being trampled underfoot, degraded, ridiculed, and then dying for one's principles, which the greatest part of humanity has forever turned its back on. And such a life, be it by choice or born out of necessity, is confirmation that it was impossible, that there was no way, that every alternative, even when approached cautiously, with eyes full of hope and awe, is doomed to be overlooked; it is superfluous and in fact unnecessary.

Did I know that already back then in Kraków as I watched the foggy October mornings through the window of a skyscraper hotel? Of course. Melancholy and hopelessness emanated from the walls around me, from the cheap furnishings, and despite that assault on any optimism, I wanted to believe in a better tomorrow that comes in the form of a grand and old-fashioned, avant-garde and traditional revolution of the spirit. It would be made of the stuff of art, philosophy and literature, take the stage monumentally and regenerate everything around it profoundly, like the Four Horsemen of the Apocalypse who would come not to destroy, but to recreate and transform.

However, this revolution didn't occur. On the contrary: shortly after I returned from that trip, a crash and collapse occurred, a great bloody ruction, a Balkan *danse macabre* with a lot of mixed meat: Orthodox, Muslim, Catholic... I came back to a ball of vampires as if Poland had been a dress rehearsal, because what my imagination brushed there — the roamings of my inexperienced, naive and still childish spirit — was actually happening here in real life, in physical reality, and here I was not only an intuitive seer with a somewhat hazy but still poetic gift, but I became one of the real actors, one of those perhaps at risk of being gunned down, branded or expelled, or if that didn't literally happen to me I was able to observe it happening to others firsthand, to those around me, and if it happened to them, then in a way it happened to me too because I was neither willing nor able to remain aloof; I was no candidate for a position of privilege, not because it wasn't attainable and possible for me, but because it wasn't inherent, in other words, it didn't fit into my internal system.

That's how it was with Kraków, you see, in the olden days when the shops were empty, when far and wide there were only a few paper bags on the shelves, with who knows what in them — boiled sweets, sugar cubes, flour? And in the street, people stood in long, winding queues in their coats and the occasional fur hat, but they were no longer Jews waiting to be deported to the ghetto, not anymore; these were now different times, and here stood the so-called working class in poverty and misery, humiliated again, standing in those queues and waiting not for a kilo of bread but a litre of vodka.

Yes, that's how it was, but who remembers that now, and what is its relevance, all told, and whom can I share it with? Who could relate to it, whose eyes would light up when listening to this story as if it were something personal to do with them, although they never experienced it? But they'd feel it happened to them in a dream, an afternoon snooze, which they fell into almost against their will (yes, it would be best that way), and from which they'd wake up with a start, almost with anger, and hastily turn back to some segment of their reality, intent on forgetting the dream as something childish and insignificant; and yet they'd be unable to completely annul it, to push it away into oblivion that would coldly crush that story, that memory, like one silences an annoying afternoon fly.

LABIN

Something draws me back into that world of mine. It's a world of phantoms, you'll say. So what? As if this whole world of ours weren't one of phantoms? As if the reality in which people dwell were not as fragile as glass and as porous as gauze? And what remains of it? For some, a page on Wikipedia, a biography and a few photos; for others, an image on a tombstone; for others again, not even that… and with some of those, to whom we owe this strange world of ours, we don't even know their burial place. But as if that mattered. Everything pales, everything disappears and slips away from those in the here and now. Who still reads Horace's or Ovid's verses today, except perhaps a few pale students, who also aren't enthused, not in the slightest.

I'll tell you what I see in my world right now, and I have to strain a little — I probably need better glasses, and I haven't been to an optician for a long time. Don't laugh when I tell you, but I see a bus full of drunken poets. I don't know if you've ever seen anything like it, but it's something unique; hard to describe, but… yes, I'll be brief… very nice and certainly very loud. They sing songs, stand and recite pompously, swing their arms and pound their chests. They hug and try to climb onto each other's shoulders. Like big schoolboys, dear Veronika, although some of them were middle-aged men. But no one is so old that they can't be young any more, at least not for a few hours, I claim in all seriousness.

The bus arrived at a stop on a cold March night. A wind was blowing from the mountains in the northwest, still snowcapped, and the visibility was fantastic. It was that kind of night that bears in itself the potential for magnificence; or does every night, except that people sleep through most of them and don't encounter that potential? The bus station was bare, empty and provincial, and a bar with a conspicuous gilded bar and gold-rimmed mirrors on the ceiling was open. Don't ask me anything; I went in there and had a beer, along with this gaggle that never stopped its storytelling and noise, nor probably its song and its deceptions.

God, how many words have been spoken in vain, all words, actually — both the spoken and the written — and in the end they're all in vain, but what can we do? Take a vow of silence? That would be a shame because words are so beautiful, and there are so many languages. Wouldn't it be great to know them, at least a word of each? That wouldn't be bad, would it?

We'd arrived at some place, but we didn't know where. They dropped us there, and from the station we were then driven further, although we'd been happy enough in the last café, but we didn't all fit inside — it was a small place. There I noticed a man, who, surprisingly, was sober, obviously a local; we were met by two more men, or maybe it was three; this one was the tallest, and, I must say, the most handsome, and he kept his hands in his pockets. What else was he to do with them?

I don't know exactly how I found myself in his car. I think someone called to me to hop in, though not him, of course — he didn't speak to me — but one from the gaggle of drunken poets went with him, and they told me to come along because there was still room.

And so, riding with them in the car, I saw Labin for the first time. I remember the old, sealed road that made the tyres bounce slightly as we drove up the hill, and also the handful of handsome old houses we passed, probably once nobles' residences, with pine trees behind them on the slope leading down to the lower town, the mining part of Labin. I adore that route, that road. Its name is *Aldo Negri Rise*, and I love that black road at night and the broad-terraced houses built sometime in the early eighteenth century, with their mighty, thick walls, whose ground floors are occupied by the town's cinema and a quality fabric, knitwear and underwear shop; that road is etched into my memory from that first time like a lunar pathway; it is the symbol of a lunar pathway for me, which I started out on the moment I sat next to that man in the car, the moment in my life I decided to follow intuitively.

What's so special about that, you ask? Nothing, except that there's a lot of uncertainty in not following the prescribed roads, there can be detours and odysseys, and fear is your greatest enemy — which is why it can be a regular and persistent companion.

Do you agree that it's wonderful to see a city or a place for the first time at night? After all, every place has its own magic at night. It doesn't even have to be particularly beautiful because all the invisible vibrations of the air and the daytime forces, whose traces still hover in it, form new networks that will shape tomorrow's reality. And then there's the mysticism of invisible beings, the souls of the inhabitants who once lived here, and who, beneath the splendid mantle of heaven, sweep spectrally along the walls of the town passageways, whisk down though vaults and flit beneath eaves onto flights of steps, which in turn lead to bell towers or the border and jutty of a broad belvedere facing a stony, wooded valley that descends in erratic stony rapids all the way to the sea at Rabac.

Isn't the nicest thing about a place, a point on the earth — just like with us human beings — a secret, something we feel, but equally, can't comprehend, let alone express? I felt the mystery of Labin that very first night, and later the experience was repeated again and again through all the following visits, and there were so many…

Was it to do with the enchantment of the first meeting with the man behind the steering wheel or was it just the charisma of the place? The love was instantaneous, it happened at first sight, and miraculously, it didn't dissipate and turn into indifference, antipathy or hatred. I can still see that man sitting on the terrace of Velo Café the next morning, in dark sunglasses and a leather jacket, his black hair combed back, and beckoning me to their table…

From that lovely old town square, which for good reason is considered the most beautiful in Istria, I could see the birth house of Giuseppina Martinuzzi; you know, the revolutionary teacher who lived here early last century and wrote her rousing poetry collection, *Ingiustizia*. All those old buildings are in the Venetian style, in fact the whole of Labin's old town is made up of them, and the open terrace overlooking the former worker's settlement of Podlabin — lower Labin — can be seen at the back. There, in front of us, stretched the town's loggia, built around 1550, with its slender columns, covered by a mansard roof and paved with stone slabs.

This is not an exotic African port like Casablanca, although the sea is just a few kilometres down from Labin hill. But can you imagine an amorous rendezvous here — the beginning of a beautiful friendship — on this terrace in old Labin, surrounded by palaces of once aristocratic families, whose coats of arms carved in stone can be seen along the wall of the loggia, families with mostly Italian surnames, which today sound so noble and many vie to possess, and whose private stories are preserved in the hidden catalogues of ruin and tragedy, just like the stories of the urban poor, who today mostly live and sleep between the walls of the same buildings. Of course, it's easy, you can imagine a tryst anywhere, you'll say. It's such an exceptional, scintillating event in itself that it's almost isolated from everything around it, though everything around it — even if it be ugly, shabby and wretched, and it most often it is — also inspires it. That's the enchantment of love for you, that's the perspective suddenly created and founded at one point on this earth, that closes in on itself and begins to produce new worlds and realities not unlike those created by literature — at first glance new and exceptional, unique, and at second or third glance already played out a thousand times, just with other variations, other finesses in style or implementation.

And there, maybe right there on a bench on San Marco Promenade, is where it happened. At some point on one of those starry nights, that man's hand stroked my hair. That's where the hand of an inscrutable wizard, possibly a human invention, pressed *enter*; it seems to me just now that it's a figment of the human mind, but in another, much more difficult hour I think otherwise, and it's fascinating that we all — from the unlearned and semi-literate, to scholars and philosophers — believe like naive children that that hand steers our universe from some control panel; in any case, that hand set things in motion... and the story began to unfold. And maybe there's some truth in that belief since we all lean towards it to such an extent; or is that also part of our inner programme, the genetic engineering we're a product of?

What happened to that drunken gaggle? Nothing. Things ended, their poetic business was over, and they all returned home, as did I, with the distinction that I came back to Istria very quickly with the intention of staying for good. You know, I noticed long ago that people often say they'll do something in life, they'll make a radical move like leaving to live elsewhere. I often listened to stories about departures like that, about radical changes, but most often nothing happens in the end; people stay put out of sheer apathy, idleness and perhaps trepidation. But there are those who really do leave, who pack up their things and take off; I'm one of those, I had the right motive.

Only later did I get to know Podlabin (Pozzo Littorio in Italian), the town built right next to the mine-shaft entrance. I went to that mining settlement for many years, now of course with that man; the mine had been closed for years, but we loved the architecture there and the Mediterranean mood it fashions, reminiscent of canvases by Italian painters, and not just De Chiricho — there are similar atmospheres, streets and working-class neighbourhoods in Mario Sironi's paintings. The large square in Podlabin with the open portico and the church at the far end is sometimes disquietingly deserted and empty in summer, but other times loud music blares from the cafés against the backdrop of the factory chimney and the pithead frame.

We sauntered through the back courtyards of the tenements and watched children climbing the trees and playing football on the lawns; on some, families had planted gardens. There was a cosiness in that atmosphere of failed socialism, one that was, in fact, created by ideals, aesthetics and architecture of the time of Italian fascism, pleasant insofar as we didn't have to come into close contact with it; we could observe everything from a safe distance, with the eyes of voyeurs who feed on the images they observe, who love Italian neorealist films, Rossellini, Antonioni, De Sica; that was the architecture and the atmosphere, except that the protagonists of these films set in Podlabin were mainly men from Bosnia, who, as long as the mine was operational, went down the pit, probably without thinking that each shift involved the risk of never coming out again, at least not upright, on two legs.

Later I got to know the mining history of Labin and its environs, the story of the Labin Republic, that glorious miners' rebellion unparalleled in our sleepy, putrid history of flunkies, people who do not rebel, who are submissive and surrender easily to others because they're incapable of holding the reins of their lives in their own hands. They consider that someone else's obligation, in fact they long for an absolutist ruler, a stern father who rules by carrot and stick — a very conservative, backward, impractical mindset, which costs us dearly. I know what you'll say: the miner's experiment in self-management lasted only a month, one spring back in 1921, and was over a century ago. That's true, but the mine managers used the miners' strike to break with Austrian capital. On top of that, the revolt was a sign of resistance to rising fascism, paved the way for anti-fascism in the region, and was part of wider events on the Apennine Peninsula and in Central Europe at the time.

Am I telling you this out of an uneasy feeling that history is repeating itself? I wish that weren't true, that that weren't the subconscious root of this reminder, but you know better than me — you're the one who's listening, while I'm just telling the story; I'm not at confession or a psychotherapy session, and there's a bit of everything in what I do, even my intimate life, I know; a person lets out something they've needed to talk about, and it makes them feel better, but the thing never really ends, just like history, which can never be encompassed and described as it should, which is another of our fantasies, and often one very dark, inhuman and depraved.

BERLIN

Once, long ago, and it really was long ago — alright, maybe not all that long ago — but quite long enough that I have to strain to remember it (a good twenty years), I was on a stay in Berlin, in an artist's residence on the outskirts of the city. I was supposed to write, if everything had been as it should have been, but nothing was as it should have been: my mother had just been taken into hospital, also called a mental asylum or simply loony bin, because of a disquieting recent diagnosis, and I in turn had just begun a significant relationship, which at that point was still indeterminate and created a feeling of uncertainty and floating anxiety, a mixture of anticipation and apprehension, and the scholarship in Berlin meant I had to put it on hold; and going through that emotional mangle left me in an unusual state unfit for writing, so-called literary work. Those were two causes for suffering, and suffer I did in the loneliness of that cold building in the settlement by the name of Buch, so I went out as often as I could, cringing my way through the inhospitable Germanic wastelands where even the trees have numbers printed in black on metal plaques, scanning the gardens and yards and houses where I knew no one, where no one would invite me in for coffee, let alone for a bowl of minestrone.

I'd walk through those semi-deserted parts to the railway overpass, where a Turkish fruit seller stood and gave me a friendly wave each time I went by, smiling for no reason, not even self-interest, and showing his healthy, white, ordinary teeth, which had a certain dose of likeability, but in the end only that. I caught the S bahn or U bahn at that overpass, the train that would take me away into the city, into Berlin. I travelled there every day, for lack of inner peace, to aimlessly wander the streets. And everything was so cold and inaccessible, the shop windows and galleries; I was stalked and seized by an inner restlessness, an anxiety called depression, which was probably transmitted from my mother to me over such a distance, from one genetic code to another. I was trapped by her illness, and everything was marked by her, even the parks and open spaces where milky-skinned, freckled Berlin youths lie or play badminton, and the pubs with handsome black waiters and South African waitresses, women of colour, as well as girls from Brazil, the Andes and who knows what exotic places... everyone smiled, maybe because they were onto their third beer, or because it was simply a beautiful spring day in the month of May, and everything all around was a call to outdoor pursuits — the tops of the blossoming trees, the freshly washed windows of large city galleries, museums, district town halls, social institutions, banks, retail-chain stores, restaurants, reputable theatres, respectable bookshops, bookbinders, antique shops, culture cooperatives, art complexes, university buildings and amphitheatre courtyards, where the young and successful constantly eat and drink, drink and eat their light, energising, easily digestible meals and refreshing drinks that are served, consumed, cleared away and paid for with incredible ease, all with remarkably slim briefcases, with lightweight grey jackets, with pleasant smiles as collateral for business agreements that, to all appearances, would end successfully.

Yes, I forgot to say that my mother's illness glinted on the sunlit roof-edge of the *Akademie der Künste*, which housed prominent European figures, promoters of peace and understanding, fellow writers, but in fact disappointed, forlorn individuals well and truly sick of the political paternalism that sucked their blood, which sometimes made them feel sure and superior, other times disoriented and weak, depending on the situation and who was on the other side of the desk, or rather behind the glass, because, that's how it seemed to me at the time, people there communicate with others as if they were *behind glass,* always ex officio, bureaucratically, at arm's length, and never, or hardly ever any differently, and if they did, it was more likely to be in the form of a hysterical incident, which they later pretended didn't happen, and never, or as good as never uninhibited, hearty, intimate and human.

This is the northerners' proverbial coldness, I muttered to myself as I began to reel and stumble from loneliness, depression and forlornness, and it all would have ended equally sadly if my path had not led me to a club, actually a barn with live music, a concert where I (obviously guided by the hand of fate) met my people, *ex-Yugos*, whom I had always given a wide berth for some inexplicable reason, as if fleeing some kind of plague, but that summer evening it seems I broke down, things got out of control, maybe because of the music, the drink and my weak nerves, and so it happened: I

93

inexplicably discovered a new bosom friend, Isidora, a student from the mining town of Bor in Serbia, and her aunt Slavica from Bosnia, a cleaner *temporarily working abroad*, as the terminology put it, both dark-skinned, with thick lips like people of colour, and dense black hair. They were dancing at that concert, someone called out in our language, I guess, and soon the doors of their spacious, beautifully decorated rental apartment in the suburb of Kreuzberg opened wide before me in friendship. There, finally, I was properly embraced by Isidora, Slavica, Isidora's blond German boyfriend, Michael, his little brother with his dog, Bruno, Georgette, a black Frenchwoman, a student — she looked like a famous jazz singer — and a tall black guy with a broad, disarming smile, always in blue overalls, a dustman in fact, who, like me, also frequented the place.

That lovely apartment was a refuge, and it was not entirely clear who actually lived there and who didn't, like me, but just dropped by occasionally to join forces to ward off depression in the company of strangers, so-called foreigners. It was perfectly OK to drop by at almost any hour, without notice, without a bottle of wine in hand, but everything was welcome, too, including a bottle of wine. I remember they also let me call my mother in hospital on one occasion; the phone was in the hall, a clunky antique as white as the doors of the rooms; the carpet was red, and there was a curious kind of mirror. I stammered, and my mother on the other end didn't say much; maybe she was stupefied by drugs or maybe just hurt by the fact that I was still *living my life* although she was sick; maybe she was just upset that I'd travelled so far away for reasons that were childish, incomprehensible and completely meaningless to her — bad reasons, basically — because being a writer *led straight to the gutter*, as she once put it. Well, at the time I wasn't really a writer in the true sense of the word, nor did I intend to become one, but there had been inklings of a development in that direction.

That leads straight to the gutter, my mother told me, getting right to the essence, but she avoided rounding things off and making the point that writing is testimony to the downward spiral we are all more or less at the mercy of, to which we are inevitably doomed, and a writer is one who observes it in a concentrated and focused way, who is condemned to live in that knowledge day and night, as it were.

But yes, I was saved by Slavica, Isidora and their friends. They became my surrogate family and saved me from Berlin's uncanny cold in the middle of summer. Of course, even before meeting them, I had a choice: I could go to see Bosiljka (or Bosa, as we called her) at the Süd Ost Centre, where *our people* from the Balkans met, people with war traumas, raped women, men with PTSD in its most varied manifestations, people whose family had been killed, who'd lost everything — all of them came to Bosa's for 'psycho-training sessions', 'peace talks', 'therapeutic dance', as well as literary evenings with guitar music... the women brought freshly baked pies and pastries, the men quietly poured tea with a lacing of rum; the atmosphere was cultured, Germanically clean, measured, with no lack of congenial smiles, but beneath it all lay what made everyone go there, that which, if you thought of it, instantly made you want to yell and shriek, tear your hair out and turn into a grimace of horror like Munch's *Scream*.

That's why I couldn't stand it and basically had to flee from there. I wondered at my weakness, my cowardice: or was it just sensitivity, too strong a disposition to empathy, which ate away at me from all sides, but at the same time was entropy, which is why one part of me remained there at Bosa's, with Bosa, with the faces and bodies of those women and men who'd survived the war in Yugoslavia, while another part of me was constantly in the hospital room with my mother; one entered the nightmares of those broken people, while the other lay down beside the sick child who was suffering. It was all too much: I had too much to feel, too much to chew and digest, too much to think over and try to explain. In the end, I usually came to see that it's most sensible to leave things unresolved, not because they couldn't be understood but, on the contrary, because a thorough understanding shows that they're meaningless and that it's people who give meaning to things — that which they decide. But the ultimate meaning of all things, and of people themselves, resides in meaninglessness as a supernatural principle and a supernatural category, that in the end, we simply must accept as such, especially if we deal with all those who've experienced tragedy, and which testifies irrefutably and *a priori* to this meaninglessness.

That's why I fled to Kreuzberg, to a grassy park near Isidora's apartment, where they danced barefoot; it was warm, and many lay in the grass, some were having a barbecue, a very colourful mix of people, black, yellow, white, orange, falafel, kebabs, stuffed onions, tulumbas... I remember Isidora asking me in a naive, chirpy but not artificial voice — on the contrary, it was well-intended — if I wanted to talk about depression, because her mother suffered from it too, but I wasn't in the mood at all. It was a topic I hated; I was eating rhubarb cake, which gave me comfort, as did that superficial potpourri that I could immerse myself in for a while without a guilty conscience until it was time for me to head back to my lodgings, back to Buch and the house that workers had been redecorating during the day; it might once have been a retreat for nuns, and in fact, about two centuries ago, perhaps not quite in Lessing's time but shortly after his death, it was indeed built for that purpose. There was only one nun living there now, and that was me, one who'd forced herself to join unfamiliar, colourful company to find a way of escaping from her inner world, but that inner world caught up with her, in the end, after every step she took up the stairs, along the corridors and in the rooms of the former convent.

I was there as an emerging writer with my first book freshly printed, as a writer who refused to see and consider herself as such, and who generally refused to write. It was a ludicrous situation, all the more ridiculous because a significant other — for whom my heart was fatally beating, who was far away at the time, and who had not yet ultimately declared himself as to whether our relationship was seriously frivolous, frivolously non-serious, seriously comical, or something else, which made the situation even crazier — was also a writer, on the inside and the outside too, and like me still in swaddling clothes.

So things were complex, but whoever believed they could be simple? Besides, I've always loved complexity, and too much simplicity often scared me. So I wanted to read books and write the odd thing about what I read, but I didn't want to write them myself because I was afraid — I was afraid of *the gutter*, as my mother put it, of a life in constant confrontation with decay and decline.

Moreover, it seemed that the significant other, who I hoped would bring his life into sync with mine and spend it alongside and intertwined with mine, if that proximity appealed to him, would also have to spend his life — as a budding writer and one predestined by fate — in constant confrontation with the gutter.

It sounded intimidating, and for me it really was. It sounded more ruinous than the lives of two chronic alcoholics with nowhere to go, who hadn't found their place in life and desperately clung to their bottles out of fear, out of dependence on what serves as a powerful escape from reality, from the universe of logic and causality that was relentless in its constraints and apodictic in its lack of answers, in the absence of meaning and any efficacy of hope.

Since the only thing that interested us was hope, or rather the consolation that an albeit fictitious world created by utopia could afford, we sought refuge in writing — one of the few activities where it is possible to contend with the limitations of cognition, while creating the powerful illusion that engaging in that activity allows one's cognition to expand and grow to unimaginable proportions.

That is self-delusion, of course, and its effect lasts as long as the deception, the firmness of belief in an omnipotent and opiate fact, which has a similar effect to inebriation and can convince us that we are able to fly without wings and dwell in places that appeal to our imagination; such is the strength of that belief that even things outwardly ugly and distressing will shine in the light of perfection.

Oh yes, Berlin... they'd told me before the trip that Berlin was the centre of the Western world and that it would stun me with its modernity, art, culture and whatnot. For some reason — intuition, I guess — I didn't believe anything they asserted about Berlin. It left me cold, even before the trip. So, since I had no high hopes, nothing disappointed me, and in a conspiratorial grief bordering on depression (but not anger, hurt or bitterness) I was therefore able to establish that the city is bleak, monotonous and impersonal, that the people are cold and restrained to a point that verges on stupendous forms of inhumanity, that culture and art are axiomatic and calculated, that there is a lack of true vitality and true life in everything, that human lives are reduced to the mechanistic performance of duties (which, in all fairness, are largely performed to perfection), that human alienation and the distrust the locals cultivate of other people has reached levels that could be considered worrying, that a good many of the natives unwittingly exhibit a range of deep prejudices towards immigrants and so-called foreigners, which shapes the consciousness and public, daily life of the society, and that the cultured, decorous reserve towards each other is so great that it was hard for me to imagine a place, space, environment, urban fabric, culture, mentality, psychology, social legacy and history, a general context in which an individual could feel lonelier, and thus sadder, more wretched, worthless, insignificant, unloved and rejected.

There were countless examples of this, and I encountered them every day in the form of the administrative staff at the former nunnery in Buch, in the appearance of the officials who staffed the *Akademie der Künste*, among whom were famous writers and poets, and in the silhouettes of various waiters, restaurant proprietors, shop assistants, small bar owners, cultural workers and workers in general, so-called young business people and artists; all those human phenomena, regardless of their ostensible bonhomie and sociability, their human environment, their social (or material) position and success, and the more or less impressive image of their career, convinced me that each of them was above all irremediably and hopelessly alone.

O, Western world, I cried, as I wandered the streets, which were often ominously empty, like after a bombardment, roamed the parks where only Turkish children played, and hung around in cultural centres that offered a multitude of rich and unique, fantastically conceived programmes, whose sheer number made me shudder. It amounted to a shock effect that I consciously felt to be a consequence of that plethora, a state of mild inhibition, and it gave me the need to smile kindly, meekly tilt my head, nod humbly in deference, take a few steps back... and say in a soft but firm voice: No, thank you!

And so, in the end — overwhelmed by all those events and intents the city was wrapped in like a well-embalmed mummy, so thick and tightly wrapped that it seemed difficult or impossible to look into its soul because of layer upon layer of exteriors — I'd find myself with the *rejects* again, in a park. It was a summer afternoon, and a fat worker (perhaps a mechanic, plumber or glazier, his round head puffy, as if he suffered from oedema) lay sprawled on his belly and snored loudly on a wooden bench like a sleeping Pan in a pastorale; his head was tilted a little to the side, so that, when he woke up with a start, still groggy from sleep, he saw me sitting on the bench opposite; his sleepy hand waved to me generously and fraternally to come closer, and let's be honest, not to stay sitting but to lie down and snuggle up to him like a soft, pliant rug that he'd be able to squeeze up to himself and continue snoring even more serenely and contentedly than before in his sugary sweet, carefree sleep.

I didn't respond to that spontaneous, unusually cordial invitation to join him, but I must admit that it brought a smile to my face and I felt grateful, even honoured by this rare intimate human gesture, overdue though it was, which was as if to say that not everything is in vain, not everything is awry and amiss, there are people who understand and sympathise, who are ready to help us forget our anxiety, feel accepted and cared for even here, amidst the hum and flow of this huge Berlin of four million people, where asphalt has covered almost all green spaces and *homo economicus* in league with corporate capitalism performs genetic engineering on human minds and souls; admittedly they're no longer working towards anyone's extermination, but to judge by the cool-headed precision, the perfect discipline and self-control, the restraint and distance, the proverbial avoidance of everything that is human and falls into the sphere of personal responsibility, and the avoidance of criticism as such, they are working towards some kind of *solution*, and someone better informed about these things than me could know if, and to what extent that solution will really be *final*, and if so, if it has a target group, if it is intended for all of us or only some, and if we should consider those 'some' a select, privileged few, or should they be pitied?

These questions came to mind as I sat on the bench opposite the tired or maybe half-drunk worker (we were separated by a grassy green islet with a lovely bed of pansies in full bloom), but there was no one around me to share them with, and even if I had been in a kindred environment, surrounded by Balkan writers who'd ended up here, mainly driven into exile by the exigencies of war and the merciless, feebleminded ideology that stirred it up, and which didn't start extinguishing the blaze even after our great Balkan slaughter had ended, I'd have been forced to play a role appropriate to my age, life experience and current situation; that meant definitely not asking questions, voicing doubts or criticising the status quo, but mostly just nodding politely and modestly, smiling and shrugging ones shoulders, like a cute, dim-witted girl at the florist's on the corner, who they say is skilled and agile at putting together flower arrangements.

Oh, now I see I'm tired of thinking about those times in Berlin, as if I was rehashing them for a reason. Was it to bolster my ostensible image? So much for my image and my thoughts; they now rest tranquilly in the mud by the River Sava, alongside the desolate, sad cornfields, where the squalid wooden houses still have a tin pail for water from the well, water drawn up in a pot chipped and blackened as if soot had spewed from it. That's where it all began, and Berlin was simply an add-on, if it was that at all, and not an attempt at disintegration. But sure, yes, we should give it a second chance, perhaps from some other perspective? I need to remember Nabokov because he not only lived there but remained there, his bones fell apart and disintegrated in that dark soil, and maybe there were no cornfields in the immediate vicinity, maybe there were no wooden houses or pails of water drawn from a well, which I can't imagine, but that was roughly it. Somewhere there in the earth, in the mud that imposes itself as a fundamental principle, and with which everything ended, Nabokov is bound to have had such a thorough, deep Berlin in his thoughts and to have anticipated it, since he was a writer, and a damn good one at that, so he knew very well that one cannot escape, that the so-called flight into literature is no real escape but only a fleeting illusion, albeit a more or less convincing one, that what literature can produce has no meaning or purpose, and that we perhaps emerge from it stupider, ever less burdened by sense, and then again perhaps enigmatically strengthened and pinned to it, almost like an infatuation that later vanishes completely, but an invisible memory is etched of that rapture, of a liaison that once, long ago, was a moment of duration.

Vesna Perić

Serbia

'Fragment F' by Vesna Perić is definitely the most eclectic piece in the book. It is a polyphonic story about time and space, combining mythological and philosophical questions with the tale of six Serbian citizens who are chosen to be subsidised settlers on an almost depopulated Greek island. The author is above all a dramatist — currently chief editor of the drama department at Radio Belgrade — but she also writes TV sitcom scripts, stage and radio dramas, as well as short stories. She considers herself rather apart from the capital-L literary scene in Serbia, but this in no way diminishes the quality of her writing. A number of her pieces have been published in translation. 'What Has She Done Wrong, She Hasn't Done Anything Wrong' appeared in *Best European Fiction 2019*.

FRAGMENT F

PROLOGUE

THE CHOIR OF UNBORN CHILDREN

Think of all the children in China unborn because of
population policy
think of the open wounds on the limbs of girls and boys from
the nuclear explosion in Hiroshima, although it was long ago
think of the embryos in the bodies of partnerless Danish
or British women in their thirties, who have specific
requirements for the sperm banks — that the donor be
handsome and suntanned, big-eyed and square-jawed… and
that he have no criminal record
remember the madness of a young woman in a Balkan town
who throws her newborn in the neighbourhood rubbish skip
because she has nothing to feed it with
think of the foetuses in the bodies of Syrian women buried
alive under the rubble in Aleppo, of the overloaded boats
with women and babies from Africa that disappear in the
choppy Mediterranean
of a fire at sea that kills more migrants, teenagers and babies

near the island of Lampedusa
remember the sight of the drowned boy on the Turkish coast,
near Bodrum, where Serbs and Russians like to spend their
summer holidays... the boy's name was Alen Kurdi, he was
four years old and his family was trying to reach the Greek
coast by dinghy
because Greece is Europe
because that is Europe
it ought to be Europe
not Europa who was abducted by Zeus in bull shape
or maybe her after all, a Phoenician princess from the Near East
why was she, so innocent and beautiful, lured by sordid old
Zeus?
do gods age?
how can a bull abduct someone if it has no hands?
why did Europa not resist?
how much resistance did she offer?
who were the witnesses?
why did the witnesses watch the abduction in petrified silence
on the shore?
when did Europa abandon her resistance?
did Europa, a Phoenician princess from the Near East, fall in
love with her
abuser?
did she fall in love with him while she rode on his back to his
home
the island of Crete?
and why is Kazakhstan in the list of European countries but
Lebanon — that part where mythical Europa was born, the
city of Tyre — excluded?

is Europe a memory
or a myth,
a fantasy
or a territory?

was Europa happy to have a continent named after her while
she bore her three children in Crete?
from the Cretan coast, could Europa see a tiny island in the
Aegean
that is a small remnant of a submerged geosyncline, there to
the northwest?
given the curvature of the earth, was her gaze able to reach
Antikythera
and the bay and port of Potamos in the north of the island?
could Europa see people there, or were they just goats?
is it true that the island today has only ninety goats and forty
inhabitants?

and is it true that couples are offered five hundred euros a
month if they move there permanently and start a family?
is it true that
couples
are offered
500 fucking euros a month
to settle there permanently
and start a family?!

***

It's me, Vasilios, who has to set the framework for this story because none of them wanted to. Coincidence has it that I learned their language once, long ago. And coincidence demands that the one who begins this tale be a man. That's how it always was in my time. In my time, if the narrator came from the diegesis, the world of fiction, he was always a man, and I don't see anything strange in that, except that I no longer have any manliness in me — all that's left are the masculine endings of the verbs I use. I'm in those years when men resemble women and vice versa, and we're closer to androgynous corpses. I haven't had a mirror for a long time, but I know very well what I look like.

How *they* look is not important for the story. They're only
dramatis personae:
Andrej, a software engineer, 32
Ana, Andrej's wife, 29
Vuk, a criminal, 30
Sandra, a divorcee, unable to get pregnant, 40
Marija, pregnant, 28
Ivana, Marija's partner, who isn't and won't be pregnant, 35
Kostas, an ornithologist, 30
Eleonora's falcon, a young female (I don't know how to
determine the age of birds)
The choir of unborn children, not as much faces as voices

I looked on them as children of my own in those few months, and anyone who says they love their children equally is lying. I don't have any children, but I know it's not possible; it's completely irrational why we love one child more than another, and it has nothing to do with how devoted they are to us, nor with physical similarity, nor with any inkling of what they could be and what we madly search for in their movements, looks and voices. We have to come to terms with the fact that it's impossible to be as loved as much as someone's brother or sister. It's even worse for only children: *What if it's not me they love but an unreal idea about me?* I did love them, but not equally, and I hope, like every parent, that they never realised it. I wasn't their father. They neither sought nor expected a father but came here because of completely different truths — or were running from them.

Ana, for example, misinterpreted my relationship with her husband, Andrej, from the start. She feared that her husband could be in love with another man:

No, it's not homosexual infatuation. There's no physical desire or lust. Andrej isn't gay, but he is obsessed. It's more like he's found a father different to his biological father, who tells him everything from the beginning. He learns the letters and numbers with him. That's how it is. I've never seen him as happy as with Uncle Vaso.

Vaso is Vasilios, an old man who could even be our grandfather. He's the chief on the island. They say he's descended from a certain Vasilios who discovered a relic in the wreck of an ancient ship here off the coast of Antikythera. Divers and sponge collectors who used to go down here early last century chanced on the wreck. Statues, vessels, treasure… and a box. I didn't delve. It was a woman in front of the church who told me he had a famous ancestor. I get the impression he never sleeps.

She certainly went overboard in her paranoia. She felt I was stalking her and watching all of them at the same time. I was especially amused when she averred that there were multiples of me everywhere:

'He pries into our thoughts, so I can't cry in peace,' she began her audio notes on her mobile phone. 'No, I'm not pregnant, but that's not what makes me want to cry. I'm not pregnant yet because we haven't had sex since we arrived on the island… I've been through two cycles. It doesn't seem to matter to my husband at all. He's possessed. He seems not to understand that they'll deport us if…'

Ana was afraid that if they didn't accomplish the mission of populating Antikythera, at least through simple reproduction, we'd send them back to Belgrade.

And she was not alone in that fear.

Vuk was apprehensive about Sandra, although he'd come to the island with her. Gloomy and inaccessible, he scarcely spoke, was always eyeing the situation, and felt especially provoked by Ivana and Marija's love affair. Something *triggered* him there, I heard that expression when Sandra asked what had made him so edgy. I know he'd never live out his aggressive fantasies, but for a moment they frightened me too. *If I throw her into the sea in the dead of night no one will notice*, Vuk thought not once, but several times, as if his pent-up hatred of his own fate as a loser and outsider was focussed on that one young woman. *It unnerves me no end. I can't figure out dykes at all. Her Marija isn't a lesbian but is definitely going through a severe mental crisis. Some idiot fucked her over, and now she thinks only a woman can heal her wounds. And now check this: I didn't ask 'cos I don't care, but I heard she's pregnant by the brother of this gidget who unnerves me. I don't understand it either. How can someone screw someone else's brother just to get pregnant? It's rocket science to me. That dyke Ivana is such a pain in the neck that her brother is bound to be one too. I know jailbirds like that who want to nail you against the bathroom wall 'cos they haven't had it off for months. They pretend they're big shots 'cos you're new — pure hierarchy, bro — but they don't know you're in the hole 'cos you're much more fucked up than them. And I don't understand how... I mean, the Greeks are Orthodox like us. They don't recognise lesbians, so how can the two of them even think of settling here? They're not a couple, and they never can be. The ad was nice and clear: couples who'll have children!*

There were a lot of things Vuk didn't understand. He couldn't even fathom the motives of Sandra, who he came to the island with, and she didn't tell him she'd never be able to have children. She confided it in someone else: Kostas, the birdwatcher: 'I'm forty, but that's not the reason I can't have any. I had an abortion with complications. You mustn't tell anyone,' she begged him — half begged, half ordered. He promised not to tell anyone because we would've expelled them from the island immediately. Sandra and Vuk were not lovers, husband and wife, or anything. They met on Tinder a few weeks before coming to the island. Kostas didn't understand her despair, her frantic desire to stay in this godforsaken place. It wasn't so much a desire to stay as to escape from somewhere else.

Why do people leave for other places and never come back again? Kostas wondered. *If they leave for good, which part of them dies: the part that remains in that country or the one they take with them to remind them of that death?*

INTERLUDE

THE CHOIR OF UNBORN CHILDREN

Eleonora's falcon, with a wingspan of 87-104cm, is a light and elegant bird of prey. It feeds on large insects, bats and also smaller species of bird, which it picks apart and gives to its young. Two thirds of the world population live in large colonies on the Greek islands, and their biggest habitat is on Antikythera. Part of the population is also resident in Sardinia.

It is a migratory bird that travels great distances to winter in Madagascar.

On its way there, it either crosses the Suez Canal before flying south down the Red Sea and across the Horn of Africa, or flies through the Sahara Desert and the equatorial rainforests until reaching Kenya and Mozambique.

Those are the two most common migration routes or corridors.

From Europe.

To Africa.

The young of Eleonora's falcon can undertake such a long journey from the age of 10 months. This species is also unique in that young individuals migrating to the south for the first time are not accompanied by adult members of the cast. They are able to find their own way using vector navigation and orient themselves by the earth's geomagnetic field, the stars or the position of the sun. The falcon is named after the judge Eleanor of Arborea, a Sardinian princess and author of the first European law to protect birds of prey.

I warned Andrej that Ana could become estranged from him. Women need attention like sunflowers need the sun. She's fragile, and you can see she needs his attention. I gave her a pair of wooden slippers, the only thing I've kept of my wife, Dafina. She's the same size — their feet even look similar — but she says the leather straps rub, so she walks barefoot. After absorbing so many Belgrade winters, she says, the hot stone does her good. She often complains of headaches. Just like Dafina, long long ago... I bring her lemon balm flowers to make tea. A few days ago, she cried while she was combing her hair. She's still a child, I thought. *I miss the city*, she said to herself, and I heard very well that she said it. This morning she had a minor panic attack when she couldn't remember what day it is; she wanted to look at the calendar in her mobile phone and searched for it. When she found it on the charger she calmed down, but the attack continued when she noticed the display was still black and the phone had died forever. She started to scream that I was to blame for there being no internet on the island, and that she'd never be able to call her mother again, and that she'd die here alone. Then she ran off to the lighthouse and managed to lock herself in. I saw her climb the spiral stairs to the very top, but I knew she wasn't going to jump, on the contrary, she needed a break. She came down again in the late afternoon, unlocked, and said she was famished. I cooked her moussaka, with a topping of goat's cheese. She ate in silence and then fell asleep in my kitchen. Andrej and I kept working on the mechanism in my cellar.

Ivana spent that afternoon with Kostas, who lives in Athens and comes here from the mainland several times a year with the same ferry that brought them. He tags birds by fitting them with rings. She helped him catch a female falcon that had got entangled in wires cast up by the sea. Its right wing was pierced, and he spoke Μείνε ακίνητος, μείνε ακίνητος (Stay still, stay still). It stared at him with its glassy eyes and really did keep still as they gently withdrew the wire. Ivana had never been particularly fond of birds, but she'd never forget that look. The bird gazed at Kostas like a small child might.

At the observatory, Ivana and Kostas sometimes roll a joint each. Ivana is deadly bored here, but she admits she can be *OK* about it. Kostas gave her his boots and told her he wouldn't need them any more. She found that strange because he struck her as extremely self-centred. He asked her how a woman could love another woman and how a woman needed to be loved. She lost her temper and told him he was an autistic idiot who only knew about birds, and that there were sure to be same-sex relationships between birds too — we just didn't see them.

'Maybe you're right,' Kostas said. 'I just wanted to ask what kind of love you women expect... does my question make sense?'

Her girlfriend Marija vomited in the toilet on the flight from Belgrade to Athens. Then she vomited over the side of the ferry. Andrej happened to be right next to her and held her in a brotherly way. He was afraid she'd tear her nose piercing when she wiped her face. He thought the two of them, she and Ivana, had an advantage over Ana and him because she was already pregnant. He noticed that they argued about cigarettes and then avoided each other for a while on the ferry.

He and Ana offered her nibbles, but she declined. Later she and Ivana hugged and made up. There really was an unearthly tenderness, which he'd never seen the like of. He felt a kind of shame. She later told him her parents renounced her when she became pregnant by in vitro fertilisation with the help of her girlfriend Ivana's brother. She said she was the best medical student, with consistent high distinctions, but she realised that only shamans could heal, and doctors could only patch us up. Andrej has no idea about diseases, but he could imagine Marija as a shaman because she hummed so beautifully and hypnotically as the ferry was sailing into port. He thought back then that she was the strongest of them all and that if she read their thoughts, fears and misgivings she'd turn the ferry back to Piraeus immediately. That thought froze him. He was flabbergasted and thought: *If we don't go ashore it will be the end of my world, but my cosmos won't be reborn and I'll never get another chance.*

She may have read his fears and misgivings, but she didn't say anything.

'You know there's no gynaecologist on the island — the nearest is in Crete. The question is whether there's always a doctor,' Andrej warned.

'Maybe you need a priest more than a doctor,' she replied.

'I need a miracle,' Andrej said with a slightly archaic smile.

In the morning, when everyone had settled into the large two-storey house with a huge, shared kitchen and ascetically simple double rooms, while everyone else was still sleeping, Marija enjoyed an ouzo on the porch and watched Vuk dozing in the hammock with the huge scar on his neck, slightly below the throat. He was bald. She couldn't tell his age. She thought everyone was afraid of him. He was silent, he didn't speak much. He carried the suitcases for his wife or girlfriend, Sandra. She was older than him, after all. They didn't touch, which Marija found very strange. At first she thought they were a long-married couple or high-school sweethearts who could no longer see and love anyone else. When I asked him in front of everyone how he got the scar, Vuk said, so loudly that everyone could hear, that he'd been protecting a girl in a dark street one night, and the attackers slashed him in the neck with a broken bottle. I just shook my head and walked away. Sandra's face was calm, no movement of any vein on her temples, no twitch in the corners of her mouth, and her gaze was blank. Those words seemed to have been just for her. Everyone believed him. Except for her. And me.

Two days ago, Marija met him on her regular walk around the island. He was coming out of the Church of the Prophet Elijah, the furthest from their house, with his head bowed. His shoulders shook. It was early morning. They were alone and she had nowhere to hide, so his pain made her feel awkward. Then he lost control and started bawling and crying. He knelt down, and she told him everything would be alright and that it was OK to cry. Her hand touched his head. She felt the frankincense entering through the pores of her fingertips, an odour both sweet and pungent. She knew he'd admitted some great and significant thing to himself, and he deluded himself that there was a god sitting in the church who needed to forgive him.

'Don't tell her anything —,' he choked with emotion,

'because we hardly know each other. I did something terrible; I was in a hard place, and I will be forever.'

'Hell doesn't exist, it's nonsense,' Marija said.

'No, it's not. Think about death for a minute. Something happens when you kill a person and end their life. Understand, kid?'

She nodded mechanically. At that moment, she was thinking only of her sixteenth week of pregnancy, and this hulk seemed smaller than her foetus.

'Forgive me for troubling you like this. You're fine, aren't you? Tell me you're fine and everything's OK with the baby…'

'Everything's OK with me. Forgive yourself. And don't worry, no one will find you here — we came here not to be found.'

Andrej and I had been in my cellar for five weeks. I noticed their curiosity. They only knew we were 'tinkering around with a machine' but they didn't hear any sound, and that drove them crazy and amused me a lot. They sensed it wasn't a computer down there after all, although Andrej is a software engineer.

When they'd all have lunch together on the porch, I caught Sandra several times surreptitiously studying Andrej's face. She thought he had a baby-like face, as if he'd grown up prematurely as a boy and were still eighteen. She noticed that his enthusiasm varied during the day like a sine curve; he was calmest when he was with his wife, Ana, and he was very affectionate towards her. *But he's not there — it's not that kind of presence*, Sandra thought, but she still envied Ana. In the third week of their stay on the island, he brought Ana watermelons, which had come by ferry from Crete, and cut the most meticulous slices imaginable. For some reason, Sandra thought the unequal number of black seeds would madden an obsessive-compulsive person like him, and the way he watched and waited as the irregularity evolved unsettled her deeply. Then she recalled a sundown back in Belgrade and eating watermelon alone on her terrace because the guy she was waiting for didn't show up for an hour, two, three... all night. His phone was unavailable the whole time, and there was no way of knowing where he was. She left a trace of watermelon on her chin on purpose to fade like a mark, like a memory. But everything evaporates, including bright-red fructose juice. Baby face offered her watermelon too.

'Sorry,' he said, seeing her distraught look. 'I didn't know you don't like melon.'

She just shook her head because you don't need to explain your dislikes and fears to strangers.

SKYPE INTERVIEW NUMBER 1

MARIJA
Can you see us? Are we both in the picture? (To Ivana) Move
the camera down a bit... to the left.

IVANA
Like this?

MARIJA
Good.

WOMAN'S VOICE (off screen)
Would you please introduce yourselves?

MARIJA
Marija, twenty-seven. I'm a doctor. No, I haven't specialised.
Blood group B+. Yes, I know that's a predominantly Asian
feature. I've been a vegetarian since I was fifteen... my
motivation for going to the island? Firstly, there's no way of
raising a child in a healthy environment in Belgrade. Belgrade
has topped the list of world's most polluted cities for months.

IVANA
I'm Ivana, thirty-two. I studied at the private Sports Academy. I
love extreme sports; I was into skydiving for a while. I haven't
tried BASE jumping yet, but I'm planning to. I've worked as
a lifeguard at swimming pools, and in Montenegro. Seasonal

jobs mostly. I haven't found a permanent job. Blood group O+. Carnivore. I met Marija… when was it again?

MARIJA
2010, on Ada Bojana. I was riding my bike.

IVANA
She fell off and sprained her leg, and I'm an expert in sports injuries.

MARIJA
I got pregnant by in vitro fertilisation.

IVANA
We have the discretionary right not to reveal the identity of the father.

MARIJA
I expect we'll be accepted because the European Union doesn't discriminate against same-sex relationships.

IVANA
We've really had problems here.

MARIJA
I'm in my third month of pregnancy, week twelve. The pregnancy is normal. I love the Mediterranean. I was in Crete as a small child… I know, I know, it's two hours to Crete by boat… thank you as well. Talk to you again soon. *Kalispera*.

SKYPE INTERVIEW NUMBER 2

WOMAN'S VOICE (off screen)
Kalimera. Hello?

ANDREJ
Good morning, here are the votes of the Serbian jury…
aaaaand, five points go to…

WOMAN'S VOICE (off screen)
We're the jury here, mister!

ANDREJ
It was just a joke.

ANA
My husband is a software engineer. They're not famous for
their people skills… they have a special sense of humour. For
him, your island is great… there aren't many people…

WOMAN'S VOICE (off screen)
What?

ANDREJ
My name's Andrej, I'm thirty. I used to work for a software
company.

ANA
A successful software company… with prospects of getting a job with Google.

ANDREJ
But I think a person can also contribute to the community when they work far away from the centres of financial power.

ANA
We've been married for four years, I recently graduated in art history. I'm twenty-eight. We're planning to have children when we finally settle down in one place, that's what Andrej says, but I kind of thought… we already had settled down.

ANDREJ
I think people should meet challenges head on. I'm proud that my wife, Ana, wants to follow me and that she trusts in me. Oh, and I have a sister and a brother.

ANA
I'm an only child.

ANDREJ
My father has a brother, and my mother has three sisters, so we're a big family. I'd like Ana and I to have a lot of children, in future. We don't have any hereditary diseases. We have a healthy diet, and we don't smoke.

ANA
I enjoy one occasionally…

ANDREJ
That's no big deal. (To Ana) What's up with you today?

ANA
How far is your island from Crete and how far from Athens?

ANDREJ
I've already told you that. Sorry... we both love animals but we'll leave our dog for my niece to look after. I know there's an observatory for migratory birds on your island. A lighthouse. A heliport. Several taverns. Two hostels.

ANA
A temple of Apollo.

ANDREJ
Quite enough for a young married couple, right, my love?

SKYPE INTERVIEW NUMBER 3

VUK

My name is Vuk. I was born thirty years ago in Dorćol, the oldest district of Belgrade. Not as old as ancient Greece, of course. You rock! I grew up in Dorćol and I've worked in various jobs. Delivery, mostly. Yes, delivery work.

SANDRA

I turn forty in June, as you can see in my passport… I still have my period quite normally. My mum had me when she was forty, so I think everything will be OK in that respect.

VUK

I don't have a criminal record. I don't drink and I'm not abusive. You could say I'm ambitious: I've worked with various entrepreneurs. I met Sandra in the neighbourhood. We got together a few times and became friends. I dream of us marrying in a Greek church.

SANDRA

I've been working in tourism since I was twenty, I've travelled a lot and visited the Aegean and Ionian Islands, for example. I also worked on a cruise ship for several seasons. I haven't been to Antikythera yet, but I have an idea how we could develop ornitho-tourism. I'm not fussy as far as accommodation is concerned.

VUK
Me neither.

SANDRA
I really do have some good business ideas.

VUK
Does that mean we passed the interview? Hello?

WOMAN'S VOICE (off screen)
Your plane tickets will be sent to you by email. You can take up to two suitcases weighing up to 20kg. Please bring your passports and your latest medical report. You don't need a visa for the European Union for the time being.

'Come and let me show you something,' I said to him the first morning, the day after they arrived. Impatience gnawed at me and I couldn't wait. He was cautiously curious, as only Andrej can be.

'Hang on, so you've only got this part?' he asked.

'I have Fragment F,' I said.

'How long have you had it?' he was wary.

'Quite a while.'

'OK,' he continued after a moment's hesitation. 'Do you think we can make a model of the whole machine?'

I remember those words came as a great relief to me.

'You tell me, Andrej.'

'Um, the other fragments seem to be missing…'

I told him the other fragments were in the Archaeological Museum in Athens.

'So how did you think we could put it together?' he protested.

'Just imagine.'

'Look, I… I'm really not sure about all this'

'You're not? Do you know where and how top scientific discoveries end?'

'At the Nobel Prize ceremony,' he laughed cynically. 'Is that what you're after?'

'No!' I shouted. 'Discoveries end up in the hands of lunatics, like the atomic bomb!'

'A whole team worked on this mechanism for over a decade, with tomography and X-rays… the number of teeth on the other bronze gears of the mechanism is also known.'

No, I didn't overestimate him — he already knew that

those scientist shitheads from the museum had mapped the insides of all the fragments and made 3D models of what they have. But they don't have everything, I reminded him.

'They have much more than you. You only have one part!' he was getting on my nerves now.

'It was *my* grandfather who discovered the relic of the mechanism in the shipwreck. *My* grandfather! How can you not understand? Then it was misappropriated by the museum.'

'OK, you want to be first, I understand. But you certainly aren't the first. You're not the last either. No one knows of this missing fragment.'

I don't know if he was just pretending to be inept or if he guessed my plan: to hack the central computer of the research project. He looked at me impassively.

'And?' he said.

'Do I have to spell it out for you, Andrej? You break into their 3D model and we insert our model fragment into it!'

'Look, I'm not fifteen any more. Kids do that kind of stuff today!'

'I want you to do it,' I laughed.

'Why me?' he recoiled.

'Because no one is so crazy as to come to this godforsaken place for five hundred euros a month,' I shouted. 'You must have had a very good reason.'

'Believe me, there are many, many crazy people where I come from,' he said pensively. 'They'd come for free if only they had bed and board.'

I went up close, stared him in the face and whispered, word for word, letter by letter:

'I know very well how many there are. *I* was the selector,

and I chose *you*!'

He flinched.

'You?

'Yes. And I know that that pathetic ad was not the reason for you coming here. You could be sitting pretty in Silicon Valley for much more than five hundred euros.'

'You sussed me there, old man. I wanted peace!'

We were both silent for a while. He paced around the small room and waved away the smoke from my cigarette, I held the fragment in my hand and carefully ran my finger over its sharp edges.

'Do you see what it says on the back of the fragment?'

I handed him the artifact. He started spelling.

'K... O... the sigma is S... then M... O... then sigma again...'

'Kosmos,' I tore the fragment from his hand.

'And that's why you're not giving it to the museum?'

'I won't!'

'You're acting like a child. No, you're crazy!' he said.

'I'm not so crazy as not to know that I can never hold the cosmos. I can only hold it for a moment. A few decades are just one paltry fraction of a moment.'

INTERLUDE

THE CHOIR OF UNBORN CHILDREN

There may be a shipwreck in a fairy tale, but not at the beginning and not at the end. It occurred shortly before 80 BCE. A Roman ship was carrying a cargo of bronze and marble statues, pottery, coinage... and a strange device. It presumably set sail from Rhodes, making for Rome, and sunk in a storm. Divers discovered it in 1900, and fragments of this mechanism of rather corroded bronze were found in a wooden box a year later. It is the most complex and sophisticated clock mechanism ever. A forerunner of the computer. The first analogue computer, which the ancient Greeks used to calculate the movement of the planets, solar and lunar eclipses, made up of over thirty gears of various sizes. The front of the mechanism bears a dial representing an ecliptic with the twelve signs of the zodiac. We do not know what it could have meant for Western civilisation if the mechanism had arrived at its destination: whether even more advanced models would have been developed, whether science would have taken a completely different turn, whether the cosmos would have been deciphered sooner, whether we'd have known much earlier that the cosmos is expanding, that stars can also migrate, that parts of them can inhabit other nebulae, because the stars too have their own pathways, and these are cosmic wormholes that cast you into an anti-universe where you are still you, but different — you receive a different identity, a different passport, and then you are no longer a second-class citizen.

I wish I hadn't portended some events. I wish I'd neither heard nor seen them, but it all led to that. I'm inclined to the idea that the cosmos is not entropy after all, but that there's a system and all the lines of our lives, at least in this fragment of the multiverse, have a clear direction, a beginning and an end, and we can only make microdecisions and thus have only a mere semblance of shaping our destiny. We don't change a thing. I didn't influence their lives by putting out that absurd ad. Sooner or later, they'd have ended up in a similar place — on volcanic Réunion, on the 'sheep islands' of Faroe, on Tuvalu, Formentera, Svalbard…

That morning, exactly three months after her arrival, while they were lying on a rock in the bay, Ana teased Kostas.

'You say you don't have anyone? Apart from birds? Do you keep birds at home in captivity?'

'No… of course not,' Kostas said, taken aback.

'You didn't answer my question,' she insisted.

'You know what I mean,' he tried to back out.

'Shall we meet again tomorrow?'

She tried to sound as relaxed as possible as she pulled on her dress. Kostas stared at the sea.

'Come early in the morning again. So we can have breakfast together.'

She took that as a confirmation that he liked her after all.

'You don't mind me being married?'

'I don't mind,' he said non-committally.

She was encouraged again.

'Is it true that only penguins are monogamous?'

'No, black vultures, griffon vultures, swans, albatrosses

and turtle doves are monogamous too,' he pronounced. 'I loved a woman once. She's in Canada now.'

He looked her straight in the eyes, and finally she flinched.

'And you didn't want to go to Canada because it's cold there?'

'She was… Canada is cold.'

She got up and started throwing flat stones into the sea. She was good at skimming.

'How long are you staying?' she asked, trying to sound half-interested.

'Until October. Then they leave for the south.'

'I don't know how I'll stand it till October. I don't know how I'll stand it afterwards.'

She sighed and sat down next to him again.

'You're in love. But only because there's nothing happening on the island to take your fancy. It's the boredom. I'm in love too…' He smiled and ran a feather lightly over her neck.

'Very flattering. I am not in love,' she huffed.

'Hey, I didn't mean any harm. I like you,' he leaned his head on her shoulder.

'You *like* me… great!' she pulled away and got up.

'Wait!' he said and drew a roll of wire out of his pocket.

He took her hand and gently slid the wire over her ring finger.

'What's that?' she flinched.

'Just wire. Don't worry, it's copper,' he said.

'What are you doing?' she laughed. 'You're ringing me… like a bird.'

'Uh-huh,' he said pensively, 'this way I'll be able to follow your movements.'

How can I follow yours, she was going to ask, but instead she just said, 'It will leave a green patina.'

Marija, now in her seventh month, was in the next bay choosing near-perfect pebbles, whispering self-absorbedly and swaying to the rhythm of an inner melody.

It will be a thrill when you come into the world here on the island. I know there's a birthing centre in Crete, but there's no need for us to go there. I'm going to try a water birth; Ivana has found a doula to be with me during the birth. Do you know what a doula is? In Greek, it literally means slave or maid-servant, but she's the one who accompanies a mother through the birth more gently than anyone. We'll find the most beautiful beach for you, I promise. No, Ivana won't be your dad. She'll be your other mum, but don't you worry about that. My mother wasn't a real mother either; primarily she was a lecturer, an inspector, a judge, a waitress and a cook — everything but a mother, because I was invisible. So it doesn't really matter whether someone is just called Mum or is really a mum.'

Vuk and Sandra were finishing breakfast, the first she prepared for him since they came to Antikythera. Until then, Sandra hadn't wanted to make anything for him. He cooked for them, and he went to get fish and shellfish. I don't know, and I'll never find out what happened that morning, why she got up unusually serene after a sleepless night, one so calm and full of stars.

'Are you sure that's what you want?' he asked — a man who'd killed people in cold blood, a man who never asked a woman first if she wanted to have sex with him.

She nodded. He hesitated, as if doubting her decision.

'I'd never have dreamed you'd want that,' he said.

'That I'd want a guy like you?'

'What am I like?'

'Do you think I don't know how you got that scar on your neck? Certainly not from defending someone from three assailants in a dark doorway. Do you think I don't know what kind of *delivery work* you were into, and that I believe the bit about you not having a criminal record?'

'Well, you went off into the unknown with a guy like that, and here we are.'

'Then you understand what I left to go off into the unknown.'

'It's not so terrible when they thrash you, cut you, split your head or kneecap you. It looks like it was no worse for me than it was for you.'

'What happened to me... I was trussed up and shipped off to a distant island to be eaten by cannibals — hair, bones and all,' she laughed.

'You wished that upon him? Do you know cannibals still exist today?'

'And why shouldn't they? Where they live, time has no need to pass. Maybe they're on that *island of the day before*, where the easternmost time zone begins and the westernmost ends. They collide at a point that exists in two times and one space. We sailed around islands like that once on the cargo ship.

'Didn't you say you worked on cruise ships?'

'I did say that. It sounds glamorous, but a cargo ship is more exciting.'

Everyone found their own balance. It seemed to me that we all in fact function as a mechanism whose parts appear to work independently of each other but all contribute to a kind of harmony, like a pleasant, relaxed rocking in amniotic fluid. I only passed through that soothing micro-ocean for a moment, like an ultrasound probe, and unfailingly located my most important catch — him, completely immersed in algorithms, and as lonely as the mythical monster-fish that may still slumber in the abyssal depths of the Mariana Trench. I let him study Fragment F on his own. It took him far less time than me. I'm under no illusion, I know it's not because of my age.

'Look! The central gear is solar — it makes one turn in a year.'

'Yes, the constructor still adhered to Ptolemy's geocentric model.'

'And here's the gear that designates the 19-year metonic cycle.'

'This one rotates following the orbit of Venus. Here's Mars, and the last is Saturn. Uranus and Pluto hadn't yet been discovered.'

'The 3D model I hacked from their website is perfect, I've checked everything. There's no mistake in the calculations. This one from our fragment fits in with it, for the Saros cycle of 223 months. The mechanism predicts not only the time of the solar and lunar eclipses, but also their colour!'

'So when will you insert the model of our fragment?'

'We'll get a complete simulation of the entire mechanism.'

'The entire…?! How long will you need?'

'Are you in a hurry?'

Still, I became impatient.

'How long?'

'I made an android app of the model and uploaded it to my mobile.'

'What?'

'Last night. I checked all the codes again this morning. Here, look!'

He handed me his phone with the ease of the Creator, casually clicked to start the application and smiled diabolically.

'Well? What do you say?'

What I saw then — it was the dance of the cosmos. It's true that the simulation was geocentric and contained five orbiting planets rather than seven, and it's true that it was not the original bronze rings, gears and hands, but there was something about that digital elegance... something so triumphant but simple, and at the same time a terrible realisation, because where are we now, so many centuries later? Are we really as far as we think we are?

'And you've said nothing all this time since you finished?'

'I've never been a talker. Well, what are we going to do now?

I put down the mobile and poured us each an ouzo. I took a rockmelon, cut it in half and pulled out the pitted entrails. When a melon is cut into pieces, they look almost like truncated pyramids. I wrapped each of them in a sheet of prosciutto.

'Do you hear me, Vasilios?'

'Try this, you haven't eaten any like this before.'

He took a bite of the melon with prosciutto.

'Come on, tell me, what are we going to do now?'

'Nothing… you should eat, it's no good when it warms up.'

'I asked you what we're going to do now?'

'Now we'll go fishing for a bit. Do you know how long it's been since I…'

'Is that all you have to tell me?'

What is there to do when it just takes one click to look at Hubble's photographs of planets and nebulae in high resolution, when the number pi is known to the seventeenth decimal place, when there's a model of the human genome — what else is there still to do?

Why did I keep Fragment F? Why did I wait specifically for Andrej to relieve me of it? How did I know that one day a young man would come and solve what had been rankling me in just a few steps: where would we be if the ship had not sunk? Would the earth be sufficient for us, or congested as it is now? Why were such powerful empires created, only to fall silent after a few centuries and enter the chronicles or odes? Why today, when there are no such empires and we can fly around all their borders by plane in just a few hours, do some people have to leave their geographies and go like migratory birds that meld the seasons in themselves? They flee, terrified by hunger, war, indignity or lack of prospects, taking only their language with them, while others own entire islands, cities, and maybe even coral reefs, invisible satellites…

'I feel like octopus today.'

'Hang on… you have a simulation of the oldest computer in your hand, and you want to go fucking fishing?'

'Did you know that octopuses are more intelligent than some mammals?'

'I expected you to *eureka* about the island for joy.'

'You see, Andy, too much joy sometimes leads to implosion.'

I took my harpoon and went outside.

After that, Andrej no longer wanted to communicate with me. I tried to lift his spirits by proposing games of chess, but in vain.

Ana spent more and more mornings on the rocks, while he took fresh goat's milk to Marija and Ivana and then vanished up into the lighthouse. I think he was writing something with a pencil from my drawer in the cellar cabinet — it was a discovery for him, the graphite in a wooden sheath that I sharpened with a knife. He certainly didn't write poems, nor did he write formulae or rancorous letters to me… I'll never find out what it might have been.

Marija's joints swelled up a lot on the verge of her ninth month. Ivana applied compresses and rocked her in the hammock below the porch, and she picked figs every day, which Marija devoured in incredible quantities. Ivana once showed her the supposedly compelling similarity between female anatomy and a ripe fig; Marija just laughed and shook her head.

You know, the concept of mother is very strange. When you're invisible, it doesn't mean you're not in your mother's sight. It means she doesn't recognise who you really are, even if you're sitting on her lap. And she won't let you be who you want to be. I'll let you be who you want. When you're inside me, it doesn't mean I own you — I'll never own you; I'm just one moment your body passes through on the way to new discoveries. But I'll always be here for you. Soon we'll be getting our own house, we'll redecorate that pale-blue one on the hill. It's safer not to be right by the sea because of the winds and storms in November. The view is magnificent. It's the highest point of the island, higher even than the lighthouse and the helidrome.

EPILOGUE

I sent an anonymous parcel to the Archaeological Museum. That 3.16kg package contained the missing Fragment F — the key part of the mechanism. I'm sure they won't do a digital simulation as fast as he did, but I'm in no hurry. As long as I know it's possible.

Andrej left for Silicon Valley after all — for Palo Alto, the home of the California redwood. I like to imagine him, when he's tired of coding, walking barefoot on the Pacific coast, on San Francisco Bay, dipping his toes in the water and pondering the medieval engraving that shows the boundaries of the then known world. It shows a chasm behind a cliff, above and below the rim of a flat disc embraced by a celestial membrane in spherical form, while Flammarion's traveller searches by touch for other possible worlds at the edge of the earth. But, frightened by the depth of spacetime unknown to him, like that traveller, Andrej takes a few steps back on the shore and waits for the world behind him to nestle back into certainty.

Ana is pregnant. Not by him. I saw her off to Belgrade this morning. She didn't cry once and was unusually serene. I offered that she could stay, but she said the island reminded her too much of Andrej, and she hadn't really wanted to move here anyway.

Kostas hasn't returned to Athens yet, although it's November. He's never stayed until November before, and now he says he can't leave the falcon, which hasn't recovered from its summer mishap and couldn't fly to Madagascar with the flock. I offered to look after her and feed her, but Kostas refuses. He says he'll stay a while longer and help me with odd jobs.

Although it's only a matter of days until her waters break, Marija is quite mobile. We did up the front of her and Ivana's house.

Vuk told Sandra it didn't matter that they'd never have children, and that he'd take care of her forever. Sandra — typical Sandra — asked him: 'Why do you say "forever" when you mean twenty-odd years?'

Vuk just said: 'You know, people on this island live to a ripe old age. Just don't get it into your head to leave. Please.'

I don't regret holding that casting.

I'll never regret it.

Natali Spasova

North Macedonia

Natali Spasova's seven stories, which are actually stand-alone chapters from her 2014 novel *Запалка* (The Lighter), deal with disparate protagonists, whose lives and tales are loosely connected by one small object: a Zippo cigarette lighter. Her fresh, lively style enriches North Macedonia's male-dominated literary scene, although she is still relatively unknown. Domestic observers speak of a 'new wave of women's prose' and a hard-won freedom to explore literary subjectivism. Natali Spasova (born 1989) can probably be seen as part of this development, though the international reception of North Macedonian women's writing is unfortunately limited to a small number of high-flying authors such as Rumena Bužarovska (*My Husband*, etc.) and Lidija Dimkovska (*Hidden Camera*, etc.).

THE MOST PRECIOUS THING ANYONE CAN OWN

'When's Daddy coming?' The bare little feet came shuffling into the room, but the child's sleepy voice received no answer. It was a small room, modestly furnished, with dark curtains on the windows that didn't let in enough light.

The frail body of a woman lay slumped in an armchair, her old throne. The little girl made her way through the bottles of alcohol and gently loosened the strap on her mother's left arm. She leaned up to her lips, and holding her breath, pressed her ear to them. *She's still breathing, it's OK,* she thought with relief.

'I'm hungry.' Warily, fearfully, she nudged her so she'd wake up, but still there was no reaction. She picked up the blanket from the floor and threw it over her with great effort.

'I'll make food myself. You sleep. Have a good rest. You'll get better and we can go to the park tomorrow. We don't have to go today.'

She headed for the kitchen. She wasn't allowed to turn on the stove at all, and she remembered she'd once played with the knobs and was given a hard slap by her mother. If she woke up and found that the girl had turned it on once more, who knows what would happen. The fridge was empty. There was just a carton with some stale cereal. Yesterday she drank the last of the milk, though it had a strange taste. It made her tummy hurt and she had to vomit. She didn't tell her mother because she didn't want to wake her. Her mother was very ill and had to sleep.

Quietly she moved down the hall and went outside. She was also not allowed to cross the street, but this time she had no choice. She knew the neighbours opposite, and they were kind to her. They had a granddaughter she used to play with before she left for America. She knocked on the neighbours' door and asked for a glass of milk.

'Mama is sick. She can't go to the shop,' she explained.

The lady looked at her in confusion, then filled the glass and walked her back home. She stood at the open front door for several seconds, horrified, and then turned and ran back to her house.

Her mother was still sleeping. Once again she held her ear close to make sure she was alive, then she shook the cereal into the glass and sat down on the floor to eat. The table was covered with a jumble of things, which she didn't want to move because otherwise her mother would yell at her when she woke up; she was often in a bad mood when she got up and annoyed by all sorts of trivial things.

Someone rang at the door. She was too small to look through the peephole to see who it was, so she opened the door a bit. Two grim-looking men dressed in blue.

'Hello there. Could we come in, please?'

'No,' she replied curtly. 'Mama's sleeping. I'm not allowed to wake her. And I'm not to let anyone into the house.'

The two men glanced at each other. In front of them stood a barefooted girl, five or six years old, in a nightdress that was clearly a few sizes too big for her. With a snotty little nose and milk-smeared cheeks, but with the piercing blue eyes of an adult.

One of the men pulled out his police badge, but the girl didn't waver — she stood firmly by her decision. The other man took out a kind of radio and moved aside, far enough so the girl wouldn't be able to hear what he spoke into it.

They tried to explain to her once more that they were good people, the sort everyone lets into their homes, and that the rules didn't apply to them, but the girl knew she'd be in big trouble if she didn't obey her mother's rules. There were no exceptions to those rules.

In the end, the policemen's patience wore thin. They shoved her away from the door and entered, covering their noses.

Terrified, the girl ran up to her room, hid under the bed, and started to rummage through the box there. Her whole body shook and she started to cry, but she quickly gave herself a jolt when she remembered that wasn't allowed either. *No crying!* Finally, among all the worthless things at the bottom of the box she found what she was looking for.

A lighter.

But no ordinary lighter.

She pressed it to her body and her fear suddenly vanished.

***

She woke up in her dark room paralysed with fear, and she didn't dare to make a sound. Exactly one year earlier, she'd

151

had the same nightmare: a man without a head was following her and she had nowhere to run. The first time, she told her mother about the nightmare and was given a sound beating — she'd unwittingly given away that she'd been watching films she wasn't allowed to. She knew she had to keep quiet about it this time. But her room was very scary, so she snuck into the living room on her tiptoes.

Her father was still awake. What a relief! She ran and nestled up to him in front of the telly. She didn't admit anything until he gave her a firm promise she wouldn't get into trouble, and then she told him about the film with the man without a head, whom no gun could kill.

'And now he's following me. No one can see him because he hides in my wardrobe.'

They went and checked the wardrobes together, but to no avail — the man could make himself invisible.

Then her father fumbled around in his pocket and produced the magic lighter.

'This is the most precious thing anyone can ever own. It was given to me by a great wizard and is the most powerful weapon in the world. I'll put it under your bed and no monsters will ever be able to come near you,' her father told her.

'Can it make me invisible?' her eyes lit up.

'Ha, of course. I told you it was magic. You just have to hold it tight enough and wish really, really hard for something, and it will make that wish come true.'

She slept peacefully that night. The man without a head never appeared in her dreams again. But neither did her father appear again in her life.

***

She heard the men come into her room. She listened to their steps and their voices. They asked themselves where she was, and she just smiled. She was invisible; they wouldn't find her, so they'd give up and leave.

She could tell from the steps that there were several people in the room now, not just the two men. Suddenly, one of them looked under the bed and fixed his terrible dark eyes on her. She was startled for a moment, but then it occurred to her that she was actually invisible. She pressed the lighter to herself and smiled contentedly.

'What are you holding there, girl?'

She said nothing. This was impossible. She was invisible. If she kept silent, they'd all go away.

'May I see?' the voice sounded friendly, but still she didn't move. Perhaps she wasn't squeezing the lighter hard enough? Or not wishing properly? She shut her eyes and wished again as hard as she could that she was invisible! Her arms hurt, but she didn't give up.

All of a sudden she felt someone lift her into the air. She didn't resist but just gripped the lighter hard with both hands and repeated to herself, 'I want to be invisible! I want to be invisible!'

They carried her out of the house and sat her down beside a woman with a pleasant voice who also tried to talk with her. She opened her eyes for a moment, long enough to see her pleasant face, and then she returned to the lighter. It had to work — her father had said it would. And her father never,

ever lied!

The woman gave up her attempts and just stayed sitting next to her in silence. As she expected, after half an hour's exertion the girl finally fell asleep.

The poor thing, she thought as she carried the little urchin to the waiting taxi. She didn't notice the lighter that fell from the girl's limp hands onto the back seat. When they got out, the taxi driver called to her:

'Missus, you've forgotten your lighter!'

'I don't smoke,' she replied over her shoulder and walked into the city orphanage.

The next morning, the newspaper headlines screamed:

FIVE-YEAR-OLD LEFT ALONE FOR A WEEK WITH CORPSE OF HEROIN-OVERDOSED MOTHER

Everyone felt sorry for the girl, who just one year earlier had lost her father in a road accident.

THE TAXI DRIVER, THE CHILD AND ANGELA

The taxi driver was a middle-aged man, whose sweat-stained shirt and balding head made him fit the stereotype of his occupation perfectly.

He could boast about having seen a lot of spicy things in his many years behind the steering wheel. He'd driven a few starlets, twice he'd conveyed stark naked people (one was a lover who had escaped out the window, the other was just a nutter), and naturally, he'd made small talk countless times — about the weather, the rain, the snow and the unbearable heat. On several occasions female passengers had offered him certain services, instead of money, to pay for the taxi ride. He never accepted: there had always only been one woman for him — Angela.

He was never overly attentive to her. He traditionally bought her a red rose on the 8th of March and some expensive jewellery for her birthday. As pricey as his budget could afford.

Like every typical man, he didn't remember the exact date they met. Or when they married. Their anniversary was just another ordinary day, on which his Angela brought him breakfast in bed. Then he knew he had to speak the magic words, 'Happy anniversary, darling!' and get sex in the morning, and it was always good. They didn't give each other presents for their anniversary.

Still, it was she that he was living for.

She was the most beautiful woman in the world. He could swear that the kilos she'd put on over the last few years and which accumulated on her hips just made her look more feminine. And only she could almost resemble a sexy heroine straight out of an action film, after she'd cleaned all the windows in the house and scrubbed all the floors, in her home tracksuit and with beads of perspiration on her forehead.

She could cook better than all the star chefs and her clothes smelt of spring, such that when they began living together his started to smell like that too.

That made him happy because he took her scent with him everywhere.

But he never told her those things. He assumed she knew.

Angela wanted to have children. He agreed.

They tried to get pregnant for a whole year. When sex became an obligation and they realised they couldn't enjoy it any more under that pressure, they decided to consult a doctor.

Everything was alright.

But another year passed and Angela still didn't conceive.

That day, the taxi driver responded to the first call and an ugly woman got into the car with a small child sleeping in her arms.

'As fast as you can,' she asked him. 'If the little one here wakes up we could be in for trouble.'

He glanced at her in surprise but said nothing, it was better not to ask. Over the years he'd heard more than enough drunken confessions of teenagers, frustrated stories of women who don't have friends to share them with, and problems of unaspiring men who always blame others for their lack of success.

But the woman told him about the girl after all. She happened to be one of those women who doesn't have enough friends, and those she had didn't want to hear heartrending stories about a waif left alone in the world. They all had their own problems, which they tried not to think about while they drank their coffee, and they sought company whose upbeat conversations would help them to escape, if only for half an hour.

'Sorry to hear it. What can I say... what's her name?' the taxi driver didn't know exactly what words should come after such a tragic story.

'I don't know,' the woman replied, now indifferent. Her attention was distracted by her mobile phone and some inconsequential work-related message.

A thought passed through his mind for just a fraction of a second. Like when you think of something impossible and then discard it straightaway out of fear you're devoting too much time to it.

But the thought comes back again, this time with some arguments that would make it possible, so you give it a few more seconds before discarding it.

The third time, it comes with the hope that it can be put into effect, and it rouses the desire in you and obsesses you, if only for a minute. You want it now, you're not afraid to say it aloud, and you believe it's possible and true.

The taxi driver never understood what made him imagine

that little girl nestled between him and Angela in their bed. Or why he heard her laughter so vividly when he piggybacked her. He also imagined Angela combing the fair hair on the girl's little head and then drinking pretend tea with her dolls.

He knew then that he also wanted a child. Angela just needed to agree.

He tried to find out a bit more from the woman about the procedure for adopting children, but she was no longer in the mood for talking about the matter, so she told him where he could go to get information.

When he'd set them down, he signed off on the two-way radio, removed the taxi sign from the roof and headed straight home. There was still half an hour before Angela would wake up and start getting ready for work.

It wasn't Angela's birthday that day, but when he passed a flower shop he bought a red rose. When he got home, he made a ludicrous attempt at breakfast and took it to the bed for her. He woke her, and as she was trying to grasp what was going on, he told her she was the most beautiful woman in the world and the only one for him. After breakfast they had morning sex for the first time in a long, long while. A new start, that was just what they needed.

Adoption? Angela wanted a day to think it through. She was excited, but she didn't want to rush things. The taxi driver agreed, and he could see in her eyes that she was already considering turning the study into the child's bedroom.

He went back to work overjoyed. He didn't charge passengers for their ride until he realised he needed to be saving for his daughter's education. He even came up with a name — she'd be called Klara, after his mother. Angela would be sure to agree.

As he was walking home, he decided to buy a pair of earrings for Angela. Not so expensive, of course, because of the cost of Klara's education.

The house was empty. Angela was gone, together with her suitcases and everything she'd ever brought there, along with the smell of spring. Only a sheet of paper, with her impeccable handwriting, was attached to the fridge with the magnet they'd bought together on their first holiday in Greece.

He spent the next three hours reading and rereading her words. She wrote that she was no longer happy and in love, and that she had to leave. She apologised and asked his forgiveness.

A bouquet of beautifully composed words. Angela had always had a talent for writing.

He fumbled in his pocket and found the lighter. He didn't smoke and never had a lighter on him, but somehow it had magically appeared on the back seat of his car that day. He didn't drink either, but a second bottle he'd emptied stood next to him that evening. He didn't know what kind of alcohol he'd drunk, but it didn't matter — it was enough to muddle his thoughts, but at the same time to make the situation clear to him.

He opened a third bottle and poured it slowly over the bed, on the side where Angela slept. Then he set fire to her letter and threw it onto the bed, as calmly as if he was making a sandwich for himself to take to work.

Then he flung the lighter through the window and let out an animal bellow. The veins on his neck stood out, his face flushed, he ran out of breath and fell to his knees.

He stumbled out of the house with the last of his strength, not knowing where to go. He only hoped that when he came back, if he came back, there would be nothing left but ash.

ONE OF MANY

The Great Gatsby chose his nickname from a book he'd never read. It simply sounded right — grandiose and threatening, as if it were made for the work he did.

A shame no one ever called him that. He was just one of many, short and clear — Jay. Every neighbourhood had a few people by the name of Jay. All his 'associates' called each other that. He was constantly correcting them in the beginning, 'I'm not Jay, I'm the Great Gatsby,' but after the first year he gave up. Besides, not everyone had to know. He knew he was great — greater than all of them. And that was enough.

He was a short, stocky man, and it looked as if his small head came straight out of his shoulders. But he didn't have a scary face; on the contrary, he had quite a pleasant set of features, and he hated that about himself. He didn't look at all like the terrifying criminals from films, but maybe that's how he managed to fit into those circles so easily.

He grew up in an impoverished family with his father, who always reeked of cheap brandy and cried a lot. His mother had died when he was born. 'She saved herself,' his father said to him when they last saw each other. The Great Gatsby was thirteen when he beat up his father and drove him out of the house. He never regretted it. For him, his father and mother were weak. The world is ruled by the strong.

And he was one of them.

He never finished school. The streets were always the best teacher for him. He started there as a courier for the local drug dealer. He met the consumers and did simple exchange. He never had problems with the police — it was hard to harbour any suspicions about that innocuous figure, and no one bothered the 'small fry'. They went for the big fish, like the Jay for whom he worked, and they were often caught. So he became the new Jay.

Working with drugs is a tough business, like every other. You have unfair competitors, issues with marketing and the quality of merchandise, and you have people working for you over whom you have to assert your authority. The Great Gatsby loved every minute of it. He was ambitious, he expanded his business and began to take in more neighbourhoods.

He turned the cellar of his father's house into a small bar where his clients and partners gathered and sampled everything before it went to the buyers.

One day, another Jay came to see him, the one who protected the girls working on the streets. They made a deal, and from then on other things could also be sampled in his cellar bar. This Jay was well protected, so all the inspectors and police officers turned a blind eye in the area, and neighbours who complained were sorted out by him personally.

'It's much harder to complain with a broken jaw,' he recounted proudly, constantly flipping the top of a lighter. He'd found it on the street the same day as Jay offered him a share of his business, and in time this developed into a habit that got on everyone's nerves, but no one ever complained.

His income steadily increased. He moved into a big new apartment, bought a car and began to wear clothes more expensive than the annual pay of ordinary, weak people. Many other Jays warned him that he was beginning to stand out and thus draw attention to himself. But he was the Great Gatsby, he wanted that attention more than anything else, and finally, for the first time in his life, he began to see fear in others' eyes, and that sent him into complete ecstasy!

His appetites grew, so he leased several more premises and turned them into special bars. He gave shelter and work to many young girls who had lost their way in life and he considered he was doing a good thing. He was humane, he was great and formidable — he was one rung below God!

He had incredible business talent. He knew exactly which Jay to associate with, and which to eliminate as a go-between. He created a perfect, excellently functioning fortress, and he did it all by himself, without anyone's help! He built the bridges he strode over, he himself employed the girls he shared his bed with… and he himself lost everything he once gained.

He looked back on his whole life like a film projected onto the wall opposite, in the empty cellar of his father's house. Maybe it was from the strange cocktail of colourful pills and alcohol, or perhaps he was simply losing his mind.

He watched the last scene on the wall: the chief Jay came to visit. There was news, another Jay was keen on his business. Either he left everything or they'd leave him. Oh, the Great Gatsby knew very well what that meant. All at once, he too became small and weak, like his father, and tears welled up in his eyes.

'Everything?' he asked almost with a whimper.

'You can keep this hole — the house with the cellar,' the chief Jay said to him with a smirk as he went out of the door with the lighter. He'd taken it as soon as he came in; its sound really annoyed him. He threw it into a bush as he walked back to his car.

He watched all the events of the imaginary film on the wall again and again until he lost consciousness. When he woke up, with foam on his lips and a splitting headache, he gritted his teeth and let out a sad sound like a whining dog:

'I'm strong... I'm the Great Gatsby... I can take it.'

And until the end of his life the fingers of his right hand kept playing with the top of the imaginary lighter.

THE FIRST MOVE TOWARDS CHECKMATE

A miniature park with two or three benches, a pair of swings and a small wooden table, where pensioners sit and play chess every day — one of those little neighbourhood commons that used to be in front of every residential building. Ever since high-rise blocks have begun springing up like mushrooms after the rain, these little parks have become a rarity.

It was midnight on a summer evening — when it's most beautiful, Maja concluded. Only in the summertime, when the watch's hands greet each other at their midnight passing, do you get that perfect blend of darkness and warmth, nor do you have to wait too long to see the sunrise. Just four or five hours. Quite enough.

But that would be too clichéd, she thought, and decided all this had to end sooner, before those first rays that make you squint. There, on the little chess table, she'd made her first move when just three years old. On the lap of her grandfather, the best chess player in the neighbourhood.

'This won't do at all; the little one is helping you. You can't win without her,' his opponent quipped and laughed loudly.

Maja remembered that moment as if it was yesterday. Her first chess move, and later her first victory. All she did that day was move a pawn. But it helped someone, and her grandfather won thanks to her! After that she sat on his lap every day and always moved the first pawn. And her grandfather always won.

Back then she realised for the first time that she was important in this world — she could change things.

Now, sitting on the bench, she just smiled. Her grandfather was to blame. He started it all. It was no coincidence that she'd chosen this park. Here, where everything started, it ought to end.

The two swings hung peacefully. She wanted at least one of them to move a little and creak — that would be so fitting right now — sadly and nostalgically, to remind her of the day she found Jacky.

Jacky was a little puppy she had saved from the neighbourhood bullies. We all know kids like that — the loudest and roughest, usually from problem families, with a real destructive streak. Maja always thought they were far more dangerous than all the adult thugs and muggers. Children's viciousness is just as genuine as adults', and their psychopathic traits don't go away over the years; people simply learn to conceal them.

Jacky was whimpering pitifully, and it broke Maja's heart. At one point she couldn't stand it any more, and the sincere instinct to help and do the right thing suppressed her fear of the bullies. She pushed her way through them, grabbed the puppy, and they fled together. The dog was faster. The roughnecks caught Maja and beat her black and blue. But so what — it wasn't so terrible. Nor was it terrible that the bashings went on for weeks and months whenever they saw her. What counted was that she'd made a difference. She'd saved the life of a dog, and it was worth more than that of many humans she knew.

Her contemplation was interrupted by the local drunk. He staggered past without noticing her in the dark and crashed onto the bench opposite. If it had been anyone else, she would have been frightened. But no one was afraid of Smalley. He slept in the cellars of their apartment buildings, lived on people's charity, and bought himself brandy with the proceeds of his begging. Sometimes he got his ration 'on the slate' at the local shop — they trusted him there and knew he was an honest drunk who always repaid his debts.

One such evening, many years earlier, she had been sitting on this bench with her first boyfriend. He gave her chocolate, and she didn't know it was actually stolen. That was the greatest love in the world. He even took her with him to the local amusement hall and let her sit next to him while he played video games with his buddies. None of them took their girlfriends with them, only him. That was a real distinction and made her special in the neighbourhood — she felt just like she did when she'd been the only child sitting with the pensioners, watching them play chess and sometimes allowed to move one of the pieces.

The two of them were sitting alone. He was drooling on a bottle of beer that he'd managed to smuggle from home. He proudly held the bottle in one hand, his other arm was around her, and when someone passed nearby he always spoke a bit louder to gain their attention.

Along came drunken Smalley and, as usual, collapsed onto the bench and fell asleep.

Her boyfriend was thirteen — big enough to want to prove himself a man but still so weedy that he chose the most cowardly way of doing it.

'Piss off, you creep! I'm here with my girlfriend, and you stink!' he provoked, standing up tall and puffing out his chest like a rooster.

But Smalley was fast asleep. The alcohol had taken hold of him. He breathed heavily and lay on the bench like a log. And he snored — a very distinctive kind of snoring, Maja recalled, now listening to the same sound once again.

'Hey, I'm talking to you, get lost!' her boyfriend yelled and went up to him.

'Leave him alone, he's not bothering me,' Maja tried to say but was rudely interrupted:

'Shut yer trap! I'll decide if I'm going to leave him alone or not!'

He grabbed Smalley's weak, gangly body with both hands and pushed him off the bench. Smalley plumped heavily to the ground, then rolled over and started to moan:

'Oh, leave off it, kid, I ain't bothering you. OK, I'm going.' He tried to stand up but reeled and landed on the ground again, on his bottom.

'Kid? Me, a kid? Move it, you stupid alkie. Get out of my sight! Do you hear? I'll show you 'kid'!' he yelled furiously and started to kick him. Smalley couldn't get up, he groaned and begged him to stop, but the pleas came out as a garbled murmur, perhaps because of the alcohol, or the pain. Or both.

All at once, Maja got up and went to him. Her boyfriend stopped his kicking and turned toward her, amazed by her defiance:

'Didn't I tell you...' he blurted, but he never finished what he was going to say. A sharp slap cut across his pimply cheek, and he just stood there with his mouth half open. Words failed him as he looked into Maja's piercing dark eyes. He'd certainly never forget that look, she smiled as she recalled the 'strong man' taking fright and bolting, and he never mentioned that evening again. She helped Smalley back to the bench, and he muttered, 'I knew you'd help me, my child. I knew you'd come back.' The next day, he'd forgotten what happened and didn't remember Maja either, but that didn't matter. She'd helped, she'd made a difference.

She took a pack of cigarettes out of her pocket and lit up. She avidly drew in the smoke, pressed her lips tight, held it inside for a second, and slowly let it out. Cigarettes are one of the loveliest earthly pleasures, but anything that is so lovely cannot be good. That's what makes them harmful. Just like drugs, alcohol, money and love.

She had everything she needed. She'd been through all the teenage phases: experimenting with drugs, getting sloshed on cheap booze, falling in and out of love with all the heartthrob and heartache a teenager can muster. Straight after university she found a terrifically paid job in her line of work, which gave her the wherewithal so she could grow up. And then one of the earthly pleasures destroyed her: security.

The malice, hypocrisy and lies of adults didn't surprise her. Already as a small child she'd been told to be careful of people, and she often heard of kids entering the adult world unprepared and that it was a total shock for them coming to terms with the despicable things you find there. But that wasn't true: mean kids grow up to become mean adults, and she never expected anything different.

She just wanted to change the world, and she truly believed that good always prevails. That's how it was in all the fairy tales and storybooks, films and true-life events retold by others; that's what it said in the holy books and was laid down in every religion. That was the only truth she believed in and followed all her life. She'd always been important and significant, ever since she was three. She had the strength to help all the tramps, homeless children and abandoned pets — to save them, to give food to the hungry, to protect the weak. That was the right thing to do, because maybe spiteful people didn't respect that, but all good people did, and there were still a few of them around.

'They should have warned me... they should have prepared me for this,' she thought and flung the cigarette away. 'They ought to have told me that it's only like that in stories.'

It's not that the people she met in the adult world were terrible — what was terrible was her feeling of powerlessness. Oh, if she had a child she'd never have taught it such untruths. She wouldn't have allowed its whole life to be founded on a great lie. No, she wasn't important or significant at all. And she couldn't change the world alone, not if she couldn't even change her neighbourhood.

So, as usually happens, she changed herself in order to fit into the world. Now she had a permanent job and a successful boyfriend, an apartment bought with a bank loan, and was busy, busy, busy planning a future together — a life just like society expected. She didn't think about all the misfortunes of the world any more. She didn't have time: she was thinking about the apartment, the children's room and the lounge room with red drapes. She'd got the security she so longed for, but with it came the cold shoulder that was necessary to get that far.

Until one day, on her way to work, she saw the two of them. She'd seen little brother-and-sister kittens before. They had been playful, running around the courtyard of the apartment building, and the little kids from the block next door played with them. Sometimes they even patted them, but in secret so their parents wouldn't see; otherwise they'd be growled at and ordered inside to wash their hands so they wouldn't get scabies or worms.

One of the kittens was lying on the ground in a pool of blood, its slender forelegs trembling uncontrollably and its little belly moving up and down fast, taking its last breaths in this world. The other kitten padded around it with muffled meows, brushing its sister tenderly with its paws. Maja heard the brother kitten crying for help for its sister. It stared at her with its big eyes, begging for help, and she burst into tears like a small child.

But she didn't stop. She was running late for work, and her boss was a hysterical menopausal woman. She ignored the kitten's call for help because she was an adult. No one would understand if she didn't go to work because she had to save a cat or if she spent half her salary on a vet's bill.

After that, nothing was the same any more. She had everything she needed to be happy, everyone at the school get-togethers always looked at her with envy, she won prizes for her work, and a week ago her good and successful boyfriend had proposed to her, since that was the next logical step. That came at just the moment when she, indifferent about everything in life, decided she didn't want to live in a world like this any more. Indifference is worse than sadness and pain.

She couldn't change the world, but nor could it change her. Therefore she saw no reason to stay in it any more. She wasn't special and wasn't important. Her existence had no purpose or meaning, and she had no desire to keep living on this planet, among these people.

She carefully took the last cigarette out of the pack. She held it between her fingers and raised it to her mouth. In today's interconnected society it's as easy as pie to find out how to make a poisoned cigarette. She knew it wouldn't be painful and she wasn't at all afraid. She wanted to leave this world while enjoying one last cigarette. Still, her hands trembled a little and something made her stomach quiver.

Thousands of lives are snuffed out, thousands of voices seek help every day, and the only way of coping with the inability to help them is through indifference. But indifference toward the unhappiness of so many others leaves no space for you to enjoy the happiness of your own life.

She managed to calm her shaking hand and lift the lighter to the cigarette. A loud *scritch* broke the silence of the park. And then another, shorter one. Then two or three more.

The damn lighter wasn't working.

EVERYONE CREATES THEIR OWN WORLD

Hi, my name's Marko. I'm twenty-five, have a degree from ElectroTech and own three dogs. I'm a weakling, and that makes me feel unmanly, and having a big nose doesn't help. I'm not very handsome and I'm aware of the fact, but I have an excellent sense of humour. A shame no one knows.

I'm one of those unusual guys whom most people think are psychopaths. 'You never know when they'll snap,' they say, and therefore everyone shuns me. They keep a safe distance, leave me in peace, and when we pass each other in the street they look down.

But that's OK, I've got used to the description. It certainly helped me get through school, where people without social skills like myself, who had trouble fitting in, were constantly bullied, mentally and physically. I was spared because they feared that when I decided to 'snap' I'd shoot at them first.

But I felt no need to run amok. I'm perfectly fine.

Needless to say, I don't exactly have friends, but frankly, I don't need them. I have thousands in my other world, where I choose to live, and it's much more important for me than this one.

But maybe it's best I tell it all from the start.

I began to build my parallel world when I was small, very small. The truth is that it's always existed, ever since I can remember. I simply sat on the bench in the courtyard of our building, and while all the others played cowboys and Indians, I rocked to and fro — and entered an entirely different universe.

I had friends there — some of them resembled famous actors or singers; I read recently that the human mind cannot freely invent a figure — we've seen all our make-believe people before somewhere — and that's probably why my best mate looks a bit like George Clooney. Anyway, my imaginary friends were much more fun than the real ones, who I decided not to mix with any more. Plus, I always played games with them that I liked, no one ever revealed my antics to my parents, and even when I got into an argument with one of them I'd always win.

My parents noticed something wasn't right, so they made me run the gauntlet of all the psychologists in town. And sure enough, after a while, although none of them reached a diagnosis, they noted with contentment that I no longer sat like a seesaw on the park bench, and since then I've been officially considered cured.

Visiting the psychiatrists, who genuinely weren't bad but simply boring, was an eye-opener. It allowed me to conclude my behaviour is abnormal and that I have to keep it secret.

Then I began to hide away, and now, since I live alone, I no longer have any problems.

My imaginary little friends grew up with me, and all of us still meet, though some of them are now in serious relationships. Recently I broke up with Ana, a girl who was in the same major at uni, who in reality didn't notice that I existed. We just kind of began to diverge too much, and over time, our love wore out. That's how I explain it to myself, though I know the true reason is that I hadn't seen her since I finished uni and I started to forget how she looked, which is a serious problem in my make-believe world — when you can't imagine someone.

I forgot to add that there's no violence, war or poverty in my make-believe world. There I'm not an IT specialist but a singer and avid traveller. I'm not famous as a singer — I mostly play my guitar in seaside towns — but I earn well enough, even more than I need. I've also written several celebrated books, mainly poetry.

I know this all sounds as if I'm crazy, but I'm very sure I'm not. I don't lose touch with reality for a second, I know all this is imaginary, but that doesn't mean it's wrong. I don't know if I created my make-believe world because I couldn't fit into this one or if I never fitted into this world because I had another that was more beautiful. But it doesn't matter; what matters is that I'm relaxed. Not unhappy like most people in the world.

It's not that I never tried it any other way. I even had several real girlfriends and genuinely liked two or three of them. But communication with people has always been a problem for me.

I've often been surrounded by people in my life, but I've never liked it. I remember there was once a crowd where I plucked up the courage to tell a joke. It was a good joke — I can't recall it exactly now — but it was funny. In any case, my attempt was much funnier. You have to understand that telling a joke in front of a group of people who want to hear what you have to say, and who direct their whole attention toward you, was and still is more terrifying for me than public speaking is for normal people. So I broke out in a sweat, turned red and managed to stutter through the narrative, and then at the end, the moment I was telling the punchline, my voice mutated from agitation and failed me. I was silent and became everyone's laughing stock for the rest of the evening. I never went out with that crowd again, but the joke helped me get my first girlfriend; she'd been looking on and found it all kind of endearing.

I was eighteen, as was she, but she was everything I wasn't. I'd known her for a long time, though we never had anything resembling a conversation. She called me — I don't know where she got my number — and chatted with me for a while. In the end she mentioned that she'd be at home alone that evening and was really scared because she'd heard there were a lot of burglars in her street. I told her to lock the door properly and not to worry because I knew the house had a steel door, and then I hung up. I still didn't know why she rang me — like I say, I'm a weakling and not exactly someone who could protect her from burglars.

The second time, she called me in the afternoon to tell me she was alone at home again and had thought of me, so if I wanted, I could come over and we could watch a film together. I didn't understand her, and I still don't understand the need to watch a film with another person. It's not as if it's a joint activity — you simply stare at the screen. How is it different to each of you sitting in your own home and watching the same film at the same time? Half an hour later, she called me again.

The zip on her dress had got stuck, she said, and she didn't know what to do. I told her I knew she was lying. I'm not that scatty — I'd seen her wearing jeans that day.

The third time, she waited for me in front of our building, took me by the hand and pulled me without a word into the entrance, where she just glued her lips to mine. Then I realised she was actually interested in me.

It sounds infantile, I know, but I had a major block as far as growing up and sexuality were concerned. Usually children talk and share information about sex as they mature. But my imaginary friends didn't have anything to say on that topic, of course. I had to reach maturity all by myself. That's why I needed so long.

Fortunately, my first girlfriend knew more about sex than me. But I wasn't so bad myself, and then I realised that essentially I'm afraid of verbal communication, confrontation and attention, but I function quite adequately (according to her) in terms of physical contact in the dark.

I liked her very much, though I liked the version of her in my make-believe world better. There was more romance and love, whereas in reality there was simply a need for sex.

After all I've said, you can tell that I avoid talking about myself and my make-believe world in the immediate present. It sounds a bit extreme when I come out and say that. I'm twenty-five, I work as an IT specialist, take home a substantial salary and live alone, with three dogs. Sometimes I have a beer with the others at work, but I don't feel comfortable doing that. I usually long for the process of socialising to end and to get home. There I can sit down on the couch, and rocking backwards and forwards, enter my world.

It's never boring there, and believe me, though I definitely look like a geek as I rock and stare into space, I'm happy.

Everything that goes on in my head — the dialogues, events and places — are all so real and I truly feel the things that happen there.

I read on the web recently that there's a name for my condition — maladaptive daydreaming disorder — and I was relieved in a way to see I'm not alone; there are many of us, and as alarming as we may seem to others, we're only incorrigible dreamers. There's no cure, but honestly, I don't need to be cured. I'm not one of those who'll 'snap' and then you read in the morning paper that they massacred a whole school for no reason. I've just found a way to survive in this harsh world with the aid of my fantasy.

What I'm thinking now is also part of my dreaming. I often roam the streets late at night, like now, and imagine I'm giving a speech to a large audience and explaining my secret to them, and in the end they all realise I'm just a normal person. Too much dreaming gives me a headache, which is why I go out for some fresh air late at night. I assume it only reinforces others' notion that I'm a psychopath. And, ultimately, I have all the symptoms: I'm always alone, I walk late at night, I never have visitors, I don't say hello to the neighbours, and I have three dogs that I keep in the flat, and which have been tugging me along mercilessly for an hour and a half now, and so, out of breath, I find a bench and slump onto it in the dark, determined to have a rest.

Then I notice a young woman on the bench next to me!

I immediately feel awkward. I don't know how to get up or where to look. If I look at her, will she think I'm a maniac?

178

I don't want to frighten her, but it's a fact that I'm sitting on the bench at three after midnight with the three dogs. I see someone is sleeping on the bench opposite her: it's bound to be Smalley. Since she's not afraid of him, she probably won't be of me. I want to get up and look for another bench, but maybe then she'll think I'm afraid of her. Not that I'd blame her.

Still not looking her way, I play with the dogs. They're not big, and they've tired themselves out, so now they all start to fall asleep around me. Everything's OK as long as she doesn't speak. I remember 'I function soundly in the dark', so I calm down again — this park really is poorly illuminated.

'Sorry, have you got a light?'

She spoke. My feet turned to ice. I don't know if she said it to me or Smalley. But Smalley is asleep. So it must have been to me.

'No,' I summon up the courage to answer. See, it wasn't so hard after all. She doesn't make a conversation out of it and I'm safe again. I stick my hands into my pockets because it's a bit chilly tonight. And there I find a lighter.

All at once I remember. The day before, on a walk just like this, Tsoki, my youngest dog, was distracted by something shiny in the bushes. I bent down to take a look, and you can imagine what it was — a lighter. That was a real treasure for me because never in my life had I found anything lying in the street, while everyone else would find money, mobile phones and all sorts of junk, and I'd be impressed. Over time, I concluded that there must be a balance, so there are people who lose things and others who find them. I belong to the first category.

The lighter still worked. It was an ordinary metal lighter with naphtha as fuel. I assumed it wasn't particularly valuable, but I kept it as a souvenir, it being the first thing I've found in my life. Perhaps it's a sign, perhaps things have started to change.

I forgot that I had it, and now it's too late. I've told the young woman I don't have a lighter, so I can't go and offer it to her now. Besides, that would be bound to bring further interaction, which I'm not sure I want. I glance in her direction, she's sitting there calmy. I can't see what she looks like, but surely she doesn't need the lighter so badly.

It's peaceful and quiet this evening, like every other evening except Fridays and Saturdays, when teenagers come back from town at this hour, tipsy and hyperactive, and don't yet want the evening to end, but all the clubs are closed now, so they keep on partying in the streets and parks in front of the buildings like this one, until some jittery neighbour yells down from their balcony and they reluctantly move to other parks.

My calm is disturbed again by the young woman beside me. She's stubbornly trying to light the cigarette with her lighter, which evidently isn't working. Every *scritch* of the lighter stabs into my brain, every next one is faster and more nervous than the last, and she has no intention of stopping. My God, this is unbearable.

'Oh, just stop it!' I yell unintentionally, the words come flying out all by themselves. What have I done? I'd better go, I caused this hopeless situation myself. I quickly stand up and pull on my three dogs' leashes. They object a little after having lain nicely under the bench, but after a few seconds they give in and start off after me.

But in the quiet behind me I hear a sniffling. I slow my step, and I hear a gentle sobbing. I've made her cry.

I stop. My heart races. Should I go back? If I do, and if I apologise to her, she'll start up a conversation. I'll give her the lighter and she'll accept it. I'll stand there, not knowing what to do with my hands or where to look, and I'll immediately feel uncomfortable again in my own skin as she lights her cigarette. I know that's a matter of seconds, but it's an eternity for me. A truly uncomfortable eternity. Then she'll want to get to know me because people don't like sitting alone. I mean, I do, but normal people don't. Here again, things haven't turned out the way I wanted. I'll be quiet and reply using as few words as possible when she asks me questions, the tension will cut like a knife between us, and we'll both want to go, but we don't know how to do it in a civilised way.

Instead of all that, I could leave right now.

But I don't. I stand for a few more seconds, and then I turn round and go up to her. Her sobbing stops, she quickly wipes her eyes on the sleeves of her blouse and looks at me.

Such sad and frightened eyes, like a trapped animal. I ask myself if I am to blame? I examine that face — all her features seem fragile and innocent. A small nose red from crying, big round eyes, and long lashes remind me of a cartoon character. Her wondering gaze meets mine, and for the first time in my life I don't pull back. I can't explain why, but I'm not afraid of that look. On the contrary, a mellowness overcomes me, a certainty, like when you finally get home after a long and stressful day and change into your old pyjamas.

Suddenly I realise that two or three minutes have passed, and I haven't spoken a word.

'Don't cry, I'm sorry. Here, take my lighter.'

I don't stutter. Every word comes out without having to be pondered in advance, and truly, all I want at that moment is for her to stop crying.

And she does, gradually, still sniffling a bit, and takes the lighter I've offered her with an easy movement of her hand.

Tsoki mills around her legs, sniffing her and wagging his tail.

'I'll give you Tsoki here if you stop crying. Admittedly he can't light a cigarette, so I don't know what use he'd be to you... but how's that for an offer?'

I told a joke! Just like that, straight out — I told it and smiled. I feel proud and can't get the smile off my face. And she's stopped crying, she just stares at me perplexedly. I wait for a reaction and it comes, though it's not of the kind I expected.

The young woman bursts violently into tears, giving me the fright of my life, and suddenly I have no more words. I feel uneasy and hot again, my face flushes and I want to run away, but I can't move. As if someone had suddenly stripped me of my old pyjamas and put a woman's dress on me.

Maybe I don't have such a good sense of humour after all.

***

Hi, my name's Maja. I'm thirty-five. I have five dogs, six cats, several chickens and cows, and a few other animals that I pick up whenever I see no one loves them. I live on a farm that I run together with my wonderful husband, Marko.

Ten years ago, I wanted to kill myself because I couldn't

change the world. Then I met Marko, who taught me that, if I can't change the world, I can simply think up a world of my own where I'll be happy. After we married, we decided to try and join up the worlds: the make-believe one and the real one.

The world is still harsh and unfair, and we're just two dreamers who can't change it. But we still keep trying.

Both of us know — we don't delude ourselves — that we'll never bring about any major change, but every day we make a small, perhaps indiscernible difference, and that's enough.

We run several charities: for abandoned animals, for children without parents and for victims of domestic violence. We provide a home for animals, and we visit orphanages and brighten up the children's lives with small presents, which we fund by donations. Every day we do our utmost, even if everyone thinks we're nuts. We've finally realised that we're the normal ones, not them. Now it's much easier. Now we're truly content.

As far as dreaming and imaginary worlds are concerned, all of that ends when real life begins to approximate the imaginary one.

For our tenth wedding anniversary, Marko gave me the lighter that changed our lives. He had it engraved, 'Everyone creates their own world. I love you. M.'

And, yes, we have two wonderful children, whom I don't teach that the world is good or bad, nor that they can change it.

I teach them that they should do all they can to make it a better place. And that they should find someone who wants to do the same. Because, when there are two of you, you're not alone.

***

One summer evening, before they got home, someone intruded into their house, hoping for a big haul. He didn't find anything much, only a small box with a few pieces of jewellery and a cigarette lighter. He was disappointed but took them with him, only to later realise they weren't worth the bite-wounds he got from the five dogs that attacked him as he fled through the yard.

HELL ISN'T EQUALLY BAD FOR ALL

'Whose is this lighter? Tell me. If you're not a smoker, and I know you're not, who left their lighter in your coat pocket? Tell me who she is. Own up!'

That's how it all began, she recalled. And she remembers those words to this day. When she wakes up in the morning it's with that image. Before getting out of the old cast-iron bed, she first thinks of that day, when she took his coat instead of her own and wrapped it around her to go down to the shop and buy bread. She still lies to herself that she decided to put on his coat because hers was soaking wet — it had been raining the previous day. Sometimes she admits to herself that the coat must have had enough time to dry, but then she remembers it was in the wardrobe in the bedroom, and he was sleeping there, having come home tired late at night, so she didn't want to go in and wake him. It's hard to escape from your own justifications: once you've repeated them so often inside, they become authentic enough that you firmly believe in them.

Like every morning, he was already up and ready for altercations:

'You took my coat on purpose. You wanted to go through the pockets and find something. You always do that.'

'I didn't take it on purpose. Here we go, the same old conversation again. Aren't you sick of it? I certainly am.'

'Have you nothing better to talk about with your husband?'

She contemplated for a moment, then sadly bowed her head and shook it.

'No, not today.'

They've only been married for a short time, a few years, but they've been together all their lives. They've known each other since they were small, they grew up in the same street, and as far back as they can remember, it was always the two of them. They got into trouble together, tried alcohol and dope for the first time together, and started stealing together — at first little things like chocolate or bubble gum, and then they moved on to stealing out of love; she stole presents for him, and he for her, only to end up stealing wallets on crowded buses. When she got caught, they decided to marry and get serious. They rented a small flat in the same street and thought they would live there happily till death did them part, and they each found a poorly paid job, which he always had trouble keeping, so they often got into debt and were scarcely able to make ends meet. Everyone knows that a love story with a happy ending doesn't begin that way.

'Even if I did take your coat on purpose, I was right to do it. I knew I'd find something. I saw you back then — you know, with the blonde.'

'My God, always the same story. That was only once. Three years ago. We weren't even married at the time. It was stupid, and you didn't see me, but I told you myself. My conscience was eating away at me and I couldn't sleep. I couldn't live like that. That's why I told you. And ever since I have to pay for what I did, every day!'

'You told me so as to get it off your mind. Don't make it sound as if you're a paragon of virtue! You told me and that was all, you shifted your burden onto me. And here I am, still carrying it today.'

Now he went quiet. He ran his hands nervously through his hair and bowed his head. He sat on a wooden stool with his legs stretched out wide. She was still in bed, and it didn't look as if she planned to get up at all that day.

'Whose was the lighter in your pocket?' she continued.

'You know whose it was.'

'Still, I want to hear it.'

'From the people at that farm, or whatever the place is called, where those eccentrics live with a menagerie of animals. I thought they were sure to have lots of dosh seeing as they can afford to look after so many animals. I saw them giving money the whole time, and they're on the telly…'

'You never stopped, did you? The whole time I thought you were at work you were just filching from houses here in the neighbourhood. Good God, in our own street! Didn't you even stop to think that those jobs could be linked to you? I thought you were smart, but you're hopeless. God, how could I have been so blind?'

She was nervous and couldn't bear lying any longer, so she got up with a jolt and started dressing for the day. He didn't even look at her. He just muttered, with his head in his hands:

'It wasn't just filching. I joined up with some guys the last time — old mates from the comprehensive. The dogs at the farm opened my eyes when I was a hair's breadth away from getting mauled, and for what? A few bracelets and a lighter? Together we looted a house. Proper, like. There was enough for everyone, and the two of us could've started a new life far away from here. We would've been rich, woman. You wouldn't ever have had to get up before sunrise and rush to the factory to slog away till dark for a paltry eight thousand.'

'And? How did your grand plan work out? Tell me!'

He fell silent again, then despair seized him.

'It's all your fault!' he exploded, getting up off the stool. They both paced up and down the room like lions in a cage, still avoiding each other's eyes.

'You didn't tell me anything, and I could've helped. I would've understood everything, I've always understood. But you kept it hushed up, you'd come back late, I'd find women's jewellery in your pockets and, God, how I prayed it was meant for me. But it never was. Whenever I found a ring or a pair of earrings, I'd always say to myself, "Keep your cool, it's just a present for you. You work so hard to pay the bills so the two of you can live in this shack, and he wants to show his appreciation. Just wait for the right moment." But that moment never came. Every woman knows when her husband is hiding something. And I knew, I've always known. So I put up with it and waited for you to come home. And I bore it all: me working so you could buy expensive gifts for another, you never being home, you coming back late at night and saying you were at work — though I know you weren't because I rang and they told me you'd been given the sack a week before. And when I found the lighter, I couldn't take it any more. Do you remember I told you that I couldn't take it any more? *That* I had a lump in my throat so big that it stopped me from breathing? Do you remember? I told you I found the

188

lighter and read what was on it. "Everyone creates their own world. I love you. M." Then I realised this wasn't a passing affair, not like the previous one, with the blonde. I realised this was serious, that you loved her and wanted to create a world together with her, and that you'd leave me. You told me I was mad, that you couldn't talk with me when I was so hysterical, and you ran out of the door. But I decided then that I couldn't live like that anymore.'

'Do you understand now? Do you realise how mad you were?'

'It wasn't my fault!'

'You just needed to wait. I would've told you everything! I had just one more job, and it was such a haul, not like before — gold or jewellery that I'd have to fence at half price because no one wanted to handle stolen goods. This time it was hard cash. We would've been filthy rich!'

They looked at each other for a moment and stopped their pacing. She sat on the bed and he propped himself against the wall with his arms.

'I was on the verge of killing myself that day, you know. I ran a full bath. I wanted to slash my wrists and for you to come home and see me drowned in red. But you know I can't stand the sight of blood. I got scared. I didn't have the guts. I knew I didn't want to live any more, so I wasn't afraid of that. I'd long since given up the will to live. Death wasn't a terrifying prospect, on the contrary, I longed for it. But I was afraid you wouldn't be sad when you came home — you wouldn't fall into anguish and cry when you saw me dead but it would be a relief to you. You'd go off to create a world with your M. and wouldn't even remember me.'

He gave a wry smile that made her pause for a second, and then, staring at an empty spot in front of her, she continued with composure:

'And then I decided to kill you.'

No reaction. He stayed leaning against the wall with his eyes closed.

'I planned it all, remember? All at once I calmed down. I didn't yell at you any more. I didn't argue. But the moment I decided you had to die I began to pity you. That's why I woke you with breakfast in bed and stopped rummaging around in your pockets. I'd already sentenced you to die, I just needed to decide how.'

'I told you you were mad. I knew you were mad. You've always been mad!' he yelled, but she calmed down. Her voice suddenly sounded different. She wasn't furious or angry any more — she wore an expression of perfect peace, all the muscles on her face were relaxed, and she sat up straight with her arms folded in her lap.

'You always told me I was theatrical. *That* I made a fuss over nothing, that everything I did was to attract attention to myself, and that I made up nonsense just for fun because my life was monotonous and empty. But you were wrong. You'd be surprised how many different methods come up when you google, 'How to kill my husband?' Women are ridiculous: their biggest mistake is that they kill with wrath or passion, or in a fit of rage. I'm not like them. I wasn't angry with you any more. I didn't want you to look at me for the last time as I was telling you why I was killing you. That's why I decided to kill you in your sleep, with your pistol. You thought I didn't know about it. But I tell you, I've always known. Everything. Every woman knows…'

'Yes, yes, you've said that already. Every woman knows everything. But you didn't know things would work out this way, did you?' he said with another cynical smile and sat down on the stool in front of her. 'You didn't expect this, did you?'

She didn't reply to the provocation. As if he hadn't said anything at all, she went on:

'I just wasn't sure what to do with the body. There was only the option of dissolving you in acid, but I couldn't do that because I still loved you, you know. I couldn't bury you because you're heavy and I wouldn't have been able to move you, and besides, where? I could've asked for help, but the first rule I read on the web was, "Always carry out the murder by yourself."'

'God, you really tried to plan it to perfection.'

'That's how we arrived at my ultimate decision, my dear. I resolved to kill you in your sleep, with your pistol, and then to shoot myself. I really wanted to avoid all the stereotypes, but I couldn't find a solution for what to do with your body. On the other hand, I can't imagine living without you. "Everyone creates their own world", it said on the lighter. And I created mine, with you, and was incredibly happy for a while. And then I wasn't any more. I lived in constant torment and without sleep; food had no taste, and there was no laughter in my life any more — just my horrible job at the factory, unpaid bills and a small, dark flat, and you were never there to come home to. I created my world for you, but you were long gone from it. There was only despair, which sucked me in more and more every day. Then, all of a sudden, it dawned on me. If I created this world, I could also destroy it. I decided both of us should leave it together.'

Deep, brooding silence.

What had begun as a fierce quarrel turned into a normal conversation. He also calmed down now, leaned towards her and laid his hand on hers.

'Like I said, things don't turn out the way we plan.'

'It didn't hurt, did it? You're not still angry, are you? Do you understand? I had to do it.'

'It didn't hurt at all. I just felt a stab of pain that lasted less than a second. I didn't even manage to open my eyes.'

'Then the police burst in before I managed to shoot myself. I didn't betray you — I would've followed you. I'm telling you: I can't live without you. But they pressed me up against the wall and took the pistol from me. Everything went kind of blurry, I heard shouting, just three policemen at first, and later more. They weren't rough with me, I just sat on the sofa as they shouted. They've put me here in this cage, but I don't mind. In the end, it's what I've always wanted. Just a few square metres, with you and me in it. In the end, it looks as if I really have created my own world. They say I'm mad and have lost my senses. I tell them I killed you, but they don't believe me. They say I thought everything up because you made off with the money. They know about the job you did, which is why they came that evening. They've put me in a mental hospital and accused me of being an accomplice in the robbery, when in fact I've committed a murder!'

'You're mad, my dear. I don't know how many times I've told you today. And yesterday, and the day before. We have the same conversation over and over again, every day. You know I'm not there in that cell, you're just imagining me.'

'I know. Of course I know, but it's easier for me this way. You know I can't live without you. Let's change the topic. I don't want to talk about that night any more.'

But they keep on talking about the same thing. Sometimes they argue, sometimes they forgive each other and sometimes they even laugh... until they wish each other good night and fall sleep. And the next day it's the same all over again.

She goes on living in her own hell, of her own volition. But hell isn't equally bad for all — some simply don't mind the heat.

CONFESSION

It's me, your Angela, though I'm not sure this letter will ever reach you. I'm writing to you because I don't have anyone else. I'm lying alone, in a hospital bed, and counting down my last hours. It's not horrible, don't worry. It doesn't hurt. It's the looks of the nurses full of pity that are hardest to take. They come into the room several times a day with one and the same question, 'Surely there's someone close to you we can call?' They brought me a book to read to make the remaining time pass quicker: a world bestseller by a Macedonian writer. A former policeman recounts the heroic deeds of his father. That doesn't sound exciting to me, but all the nurses are in raptures about the book — they say it tells of honour and righteousness that don't exist today.

So many years have passed since we last saw each other, but I still have no trouble writing to you, like someone who's part of me, like the mornings when I'd write you a shopping-list on a little piece of yellow notepaper and stick it to the fridge with the magnet from Greece. Do you remember when we bought it? We said it would be the first of many we'd stick on the fridge as souvenirs, and we'd have ones from all over the world. But it remained alone, the poor thing.

We were happy for a time, weren't we? Of course we were, but, you see, I can't remember.

It's a curious feeling that people get when they know their days in this world are numbered. It's like we put all the memories, all the people we've met, all the successes and failures in a glass at the same time, and they mix, mingle and blend until just one pure substance is left — a judgement: were you a good or a bad person in this life?

There's no middle ground. Everything is either black or white, with no nuances. And I wasn't one of the good ones.

But I don't need this hospital room and the disease that's taken hold of my body to realise that.

My thoughts were never pure, so whenever you gave me that enamoured look of yours I felt you were cutting me with a knife from head to toe.

This letter, too, comes from the selfish need to lessen my burden by owning up to everything.

It was me who poisoned all the next-door neighbour's cats. I hated them all, I hated each and every one of them from the bottom of my soul. I lay in bed at night imagining the foam spewing from their mouths and them struggling for their last breath.

I remembered how naively they would come up to me and how gratefully they took the poison-laced morsel from my hand. I vividly imagined her crying and her heart breaking every morning she saw their little lifeless bodies. And I was happy.

She had everything: her husband was rich and famous, she had a house, a flat she rented out and a weekend house by the lake. Plus, on top of that, she had three sweet little children who called her 'mummy' and looked up at her with so much love.

Life isn't fair. It's just not right that one person is so happy while others, like us, are so miserable. She had three little girls — and we didn't have one.

I hated all the families with children, I hated all the children, and I hated all the happy people!

I sat in the courtyard for hours, watching them all and listening in on their conversations, and if I didn't learn any spicy details I made up a rumour and spread it through our street, and then enjoyed listening to their domestic arguments through the window.

The children's chatter stabbed into my brain and drove me crazy, so I did all I could to spoil their games. I punctured their balls, I told them their mothers were bitches, their fathers drunkards, and that no one loved them; I said their parents regretted having them — all because they were happy and played in our street, without children of ours.

I was an ordinary housewife, with no influence or power. I longed for wealth and power, but not so as to live comfortably or go on swanky holidays with my husband. I longed for them so I would be able to ruin the lives of others, wipe the smiles off their faces, see them cry and suffer, and tell them, 'See now how it is? Do you feel, for a moment, everything I've felt all my life?'

I'm a monster, my dear, and I always have been. Sometimes I like to believe I became a monster by no fault of my own — that life made me that way. But now, before I depart this world, there's no need to lie. The monster always existed in me, and life just gave it the occasion to awake.

And you wanted to bring a child home to this monster? It would never have been mine. It would have been foreign and no different to those in our courtyard whom I wanted to see crying.

There's something more I should tell you. I also imagined you reading the message I left on the fridge, in which I told you I was leaving you. I was happy when I imagined you sobbing helplessly. You see, I felt like that every day — helpless and unhappy. And when you gave me that enamoured look it broke me up and rent my insides!

I hated you from the bottom of my soul.

I blamed all and sundry for making me what I am! God who decided I shouldn't have a child of my own, my own progeny; he drove me crazy and filled me with this malice! Those thoughts comforted me — it wasn't my fault, but God's. He made such a degenerate of me.

You were my husband and we went through the same things together, except that you woke up with a smile every morning; you whistled different tunes under the shower, and I came to hate each and every one of them; you cursed the person who poisoned the next-door neighbour's cats, not knowing that you shared your bed with her.

Therefore I hated you with a vengeance.

How could we go through the same things and yet be so different? Why was I bad, and you good?

When you came home that morning and offered me someone else's child and explained that you'd fallen in love with it even before getting to know it, I wanted to throttle you. That was an eye-opener — I understood everything and it hurt more than anything in the world. I wasn't malicious because

I didn't have a child, but because He up there decided I didn't deserve one due to my malice.

I didn't deserve to have a child who looked at me with love or called me 'mummy'. I didn't deserve to give life when ruining the lives of others brought me peace of mind.

My genes were rotten and not to be passed down!

So I left to be far away from you and everyone else. I left to live in seclusion, where I couldn't see the happiness of others. I lied to myself that I was going in order to protect people from me, but the truth was that I went because I could no longer bear to see happiness around me.

My dear, I don't expect you to understand what pain gnawed at me from inside. Malice is an illness. Don't hate me but understand me because I'm ill. Now I'm lying in this hospital bed with a diagnosis that's hard to pronounce, but I know that malice killed me long ago.

Please don't mourn for me. Believe me, I loved you as much as I could beneath all those layers of hate. If this world had been different, perhaps I would have been different too. But we are what we are, and now that I've admitted everything, I've lessened my load.

Now I can calmly await my end, in this room, with a telly that picks up only one channel, and with a lot of static to boot. I just watched the news.

Millions of people have lost their homes in a flood, they say. They've lost their nearest and dearest, children, husbands, wives… a hundred tonnes of carcasses of animals killed in the floods have been collected in the past two days.

If you were here, you'd begin to sniffle and pretend something had got in your eye so you didn't have to admit you'd started crying. I just smile.

I don't hide any more, nor am I afraid. Can hell really be worse than this life? I'm sure it can't.

Ana Svetel

Slovenia

Ana Svetel (born 1990) writes poetry and prose for the main Slovenian literary journals as well as columns and essays for various cultural media. She says that she has been significantly influenced by Slovenian female poets but notes that there is no predominant perception of 'women's poetry' that would make it any different to poetry by men. With short stories, the influences are more mixed, including more male writers and a greater proportion of translated prose. From her experience, foreign reception of her work tends to see it in a gender context and emphasise her national background. Overall, she considers that her work fits the wider trends of contemporary Slovenian writing. She adds: 'One aspect I've been thinking about is humour, as it is often ascribed more to male writing, and sentiments more to female; the fact that stories from my *Dobra družba* (Good Company) collection were perceived as humorous by many readers gave me additional satisfaction.'

SILK ROAD

Let me start by saying, straight off, that I hate my fiancé. How stupid must a person be to spend a beautiful sunny Saturday driving over the border to Celovec, waiting in line, arranging component parts of a new vacuum cleaner into the boot, and then driving back again. A whole day, squandered. But let's start from the beginning. When I first met my fiancé, I thought I'd hit the jackpot. He had just completed his specialist dermatology training, and despite being one of the youngest and brightest to specialise, he wasn't arrogant or full of himself. In his spare time, he played for the student basketball team; once a week he went for a beer with his mates (just one beer, never two), and occasionally he'd pick himself up a copy of *Der Spiegel* from a newsstand, which he'd read in bed in the evenings. He was also tall; not handsome, but nice enough, no question (a 'friendly face', as people say), a polite conversationalist and an attentive partner. Obviously, my mum could barely contain herself. After lunch, the first time Blaž came round, he was outside playing with the dog and she took hold of my hand in the kitchen and beamed. She didn't say anything, but I don't remember the last time I'd seen her so happy. 'Hang on to that man, for the love of God!' she commanded, as Blaž came up the steps. Her voice was trembling, she was so excited.

One evening, about a year or so later when we'd been round at hers for lunch again, Blaž and I went out for a walk up to the local church on the hill with views over our village. Blaž liked these remote corners of Slovenia. I couldn't stand them. And there — I mean, I could have guessed — he took a small box from his inside jacket pocket, opened it, and just like that, we were engaged. It wasn't long after that that Blaž got a permanent job, people started calling him 'Dr', we got a mortgage on a new flat and set a date for the wedding. We alternated our Sunday visits between my mum and his parents (the Dr liked to do things fairly), and on Saturdays we went to the shops. And that was the thing I started to hate.

It was when we moved into our own place that I slowly began to realise what a neat-freak my future husband was. It all started with a special antibacterial cleaner for the parquet flooring. With deep-cleaning the radiators. With washing the towels after every shower. With scrubbing the tile grout in the kitchen. Once, he had to go to Gradec to try out some new self-cleaning ovens; another time, he went to Zagreb to test a new line of antimicrobial sprays; and another, he went to Trieste for a new rug, because the old one was 'a breeding ground for germs'.

All these acts of madness did not come cheap, and it wasn't long before even Blaž started to notice that our salaries were increasingly disappearing at the end of each month. How were we going to save for our future son to go and study in America? I am convinced that this exact stupid thought had occurred to him when he sat down beside me on the sofa one evening (or, rather, when he sat on the throw which had to be spread across the sofa so that it could be taken to the dry cleaner's every month). It was then that I was hit by a wave of panic: I just knew that he was going to start talking about children (he probably wants us to conceive during our honeymoon, or better still, on our wedding night). My head was spinning with dread, and so I focused on his neatly clipped, rounded fingernails. 'Darling,' he began, 'I've been thinking about something.' What he said next was so stupid that I almost fell off the sofa. 'I think that we should advertise our Saturday journeys on *liftshare.com*. If we take other passengers, we can at least make some of our money back.' I hoped my shock would go unnoticed. 'Yeah, great idea babe, of course,' I said, stroking his hand.

And so, on Saturday mornings, we were picking up passengers of all kinds. Blaž arranged their suitcases, bags and rucksacks in the boot, put on some ambient music and made polite conversation. I was genuinely mortified. Did these people not think it ludicrous that a young couple spent their weekend driving to buy the latest range of hypoallergenic bedding, rather than lazing around, making love, feeding spaghetti to one another — or doing anything else? Literally *any other thing*. But in fact, the passengers were charmed by Blaž's unassuming company. Some girls secretly wished they could find a guy like him. The ones with acne tried to memorise his surname, so that they could book with him again (both Blaž and I have lovely, clear skin, which people put down to his expertise, God help them).

But this time it was different. This time, a man and woman of around our age got in, enormous backpacks, and were clearly on their way to the airport. It turned out that they were leaving for Greece, and then heading on through Central

Asia to China. 'We're going to try and follow the routes of the old Silk Road,' the woman explained. They'd booked their first night in Tbilisi, nothing more; after that, they'd figure it out. 'If worst comes to worst, there are always good people out there who will let you bed down in their hallway,' she said. 'We don't need luxuries; just a few square metres, and some tap water every so often.' 'We want to experience these things whilst we're still young, before we're tied down, whilst we don't have children. You know how quickly people get... stuck in their comfort zone,' the guy added. I snatched a discreet glance at Blaž. His expression had not changed; he was still smiling politely.

I spent the whole journey dreaming about how I was going to leave him. We'd drop these two off at the airport, and then I'd ask him when we were going to do a trip like that. Well, we've got to think about the future; make plans, think long-term, he'll say, with total calm. Then I'll seize my chance: let me out here, right here, what's wrong, darling, I've had enough Blaž, enough, darling, are you feeling alright, Jesus I can't take any more of this, of us, I'm done with the vacuum cleaners, I'm done with our sterile flat, I'm bored, bored to death and you're pissing me off, seriously, bacteria and microbes and dust mites are going to win, and no matter how hard you try, underneath some fucking blanket in a drawer there'll be a woolly jumper eaten by moths, and one of these days you'll find a year-old tomato lurking at the bottom of the fridge, mouldy and slimy, and when you take it out to the bin its rancid juices will leak onto your gloves, that's what, Blaž, you don't stand a chance, we don't stand a chance, we're going to expire from the boredom, that's not how it should be, in case you've haven't got that yet, now let me out of this car and out of this fucking life.

'Penny for them?' he says, as we approach the shopping centre. 'Oh, nothing,' I mumble. I'll leave him when we get back to Ljubljana. That whole scenario, set against this whole alpine backdrop, was way too reckless. Who would come and collect me?

The store was absolutely heaving, as there were big reductions on the vacuum cleaner in question, and we queued up, patient as a pair of Austrians. For an entire hour, ambient music and hushed voices from the other couples tore into my subconscious, while Blaž and I held hands, as we often do; we're still young, it's what people do at this age, apparently.

When we got home late that afternoon, the lift was broken, so we had to carry all the vacuum-cleaner components up to the fourth floor. Our arms were full with boxes and when we reached the top, we were all out of breath — well, that was mainly me. Blaž placed a box on my lap (to reduce any chance of bacteria getting into the box) and took the key out of his pocket. He went inside, put down his things and came back for the boxes on my lap. He made two equal towers of boxes in the hallway. When he noticed me standing in the doorway, he looked confused. 'What is it? You coming in?' I was resolute and secretly I knew that, as stupid and dramatic as it sounds, there would be no second chances. It was now or never. A leap for freedom. I thought of Olympic skiers, elegantly gliding off the edge of the ramp. 'Darling, are you alright?'

At that moment the phone rings. It was Mum. She's probably going to ask if we're going for lunch tomorrow.

THE NOTEBOOK

Hi there, would it be possible to organise a lift from the old people's home in Ajdovščina, back to Ljubljana, please? It's for my mum. Thanks, Lucija.

As a general rule, I don't do pick-ups off-route. But there was something a bit moving about this message. I cursed Slovenian public transport and welfare provision; I mean, the fact that even the elderly are relying on lift sharing is outright terrifying. How long before paramedics are typing in *liftshare.com* to take someone to hospital? I admit, I felt sorry for the mum of Ms Lucija. Even though it'd take me an extra half an hour, I'd worked out roughly, my conscience couldn't leave her there.

Of course! Will your mum wait at the entrance to the home, or will I need to go in and find her? Best wishes, A.

I could see myself already, selflessly pushing an old lady in a wheelchair towards the car…

My mum's there visiting her husband, so if you could please send me a text 10 minutes before you arrive, she'll come to meet you in the car park.

Ah, so she's a loving, devoted wife. Of course I'll take her; I will sacrifice those thirty minutes of my life, because what are they compared to their fifty-something years of marriage? (For a brief moment I pictured an elderly Tanja: age spots, sagging breasts, dribbling from the corners of her mouth — it all rather flashed before me.)

***

A bead of sweat runs down my neck. Where's this young man got to? I shift my shopping bag from one hand to the other and adjust my handbag. A hellishly hot day. If I put on a wash tonight, it'll be dry by the morning. It's one heatwave after another this summer. They're advising residents at the home to stay in the air-conditioned spaces. Oh, here he comes. Red car, Koper registration plate. A smart young man gets out and offers to put my bag in the boot, then opens the door and closes it behind me, too. Carefully.

For a few moments we ride in silence.

'Your daughter mentioned that your husband's in the home...' he begins.

'That's right; for a year now.'

'You must visit regularly, I imagine.'

'Yes, I'm there nearly every day.'

Silence once more. I continue, before he starts to feel awkward and changes the subject.

'Last summer, it all became too much. I couldn't have him at home anymore. It wasn't safe for him; he needed me twenty-four hours a day. I could barely nip to the shop I was so scared of him wandering off.'

'Wow.'

I sense that the young man doesn't know what I'm talking

about. Strange; with such a specific example, usually everyone catches on.

'Bojan's dementia became so bad that a home was the only option.'

'Dementia,' he repeats. 'That's awful.'

Some silence again. The peak of Nanos Plateau is draped in cloud.

'How come he's down here? I mean — it would be so much easier for you if he was in Ljubljana…'

'You don't need to tell me! Don't get me started. The homes are all full. He's on a waiting list, but for the moment he's got a place in Ajdovščina. And even that was thanks to a series of lucky coincidences.'

'And now you're visiting him…'

'…nearly every day, exactly. By the time it gets to evening, Bojan will forget that I've been, you know — but I still go. Those hours we spend together… they're precious.'

'It must be exhausting, doing that journey every day.'

'Not half. If only there was someone else we could call on. But who else does he have? Our daughter is at work until the evening, as you know; all she does is organise these lifts, and even they're at the last minute. And otherwise…'

'Are the trains and buses no good?'

'Not regular enough, and they take forever. All I ask is to be home by a reasonable hour, so that I can at least… at least do some jobs around the house. Let some air in, sweep the floors, that's all.'

'Your daughter did mention where you lived, but my mind's gone blank.'

'I'm on the outskirts of Ljubljana, in Gameljne. We bought

our place eight years ago. Large garden, a terrace; we did it all up. Even the bathroom tiles were all our own work. You know, even two years ago, Bojan was completely fine. And now this. If I'd have known… if I'd have known how everything would change in two years' time. If I'd have known what was around the corner, I would have complained less, and had more fun.'

He turns to look at me. I'm not the only one on the verge of tears.

***

As a general rule, I don't take people to their door. And I have to admit, when I looked at this woman, already of quite an age, though still in good shape — and yet also without luggage — it occurred to me that I could drop her off by Gospodarsko, where she could happily wait for the number eight. I really was starting to feel pushed for time. And surely the woman has her bus pass on her, like all pensioners do.

As a general rule, I can keep my emotions in check. I work with people a lot, I hear all sorts of things. But this… this story cut deep, as they say. I could just picture the two of them: happy retirees, full of life, laying bathroom tiles, sitting on the terrace in the evenings doing the crossword; he takes her by the hand every now and then, he slides a hand under her blouse and fondles her still-plump breasts. They had pictured a calm retirement ahead of them. Just like you see in photos in senior magazines. They thought, for a moment, that they could outsmart time. And then…'

'…if I'd have known what was waiting for us, I would have complained less and had more fun.'

211

Her voice wavered. A cocktail of thoughts flooded my brain: 1. Seriously? You're going to cry in your car? 2. An elderly Tanja looks at me with wandering eyes and asks me who I am. 3. What's the name of that film? With Ryan Gosling and Rachel McAdams? 4. Shit, you really are going to cry. 5. Say something to cheer her up. 6. If I open my mouth, all that's going to come out is sobbing. 7. Oh yeah — *The Notebook*.

I looked at her and tried to avoid blinking so the tears wouldn't run down my cheeks. I stared at the lorry up ahead and decided to distract myself by overtaking. But as I was driving up the hill towards Logatec, I knew that I'd made up my mind. I was going to drive her to her door. I would just miss the volleyball — what's one volleyball match compared to her misfortune? What do I know about suffering? If this was a small thing that I could do to make her life easier, then I was going to do what was right.

'Which is the best exit for Gameljne?'

'Oh, there's no need…'

'It's not a problem. I'll take you home.'

'You're very kind.'

'Just let me know where to go.'

'It's not far, just past Dravlje.'

(Like hell it is.)

'Great, I'll drive towards Šentvid and then you direct me from there.'

'Thank you so much,'

When I dropped her off, I briefly considered refusing that five-euro tip, but thought better of it. I didn't want her to think I was pitying her. Because I wasn't. I just empathised.

'Bye now, take care,' I said.

***

He takes me all the way to the driveway. I'd noticed him keeping an eye on the time. He was in a hurry, no doubt. What a selfless young man. A young man not afraid to look you in the eye.

'Bye now, take care,' he says to me, awkwardly putting his hand on mine.

I take my time getting out of the car, the young man is already waiting by the boot and hands me my bag and gives a forlorn smile. With my head hung low, I walk towards my door. He was still waiting. He's probably putting the five euros away in his wallet and keeping a discreet eye on me. He feels sorry for me. Pities me, even.

At the door I rummage around in my handbag, as if looking for my keys. He's no doubt realised that I know that he's still there, which is why after a few seconds of my searching, he eventually drives away.

I take my key out of my pocket and step inside. The hallway is dark, but the living room is bathed in late afternoon sunlight. Bojan is on the sofa, reading the paper.

I put my things down on the chair and go into the kitchen.

'How are you, how was work?' he calls from the sofa.

'Oh, miserable. They've given me the dementia shift tomorrow. And you know how I feel about that. I hate it — always wears me out.'

'Well, you certainly made it home in good time.'

'Yeah, he was an easy target. Picked me up outside the home and dropped me right at our door. Really quite talkative.'

'You're wonderful.'

Bojan gets up from the sofa and comes into the kitchen. Just as I'm bending over, looking into the fridge, he comes up behind me and with his right hand reaches under my bra.

'We could nip out for a walk before it gets dark, if you're not hungry.'

With a yogurt in my hand, I turn to him and stare into his bright eyes.

'I'd love to.'

ENCOUNTER

No. It can't be him. He just looks a bit like him. I mean, he can't…

A man stands in the lay-by next to the camp exit, wearing a navy t-shirt, shorts and crocs. His travel bag lies at his feet, and with a handkerchief he wipes first his sweaty forehead, and then the smooth, reddened skin radiating towards the crown of his head.

What if I just drive past? He won't know…

In that instant the man notices the large, black Espace with a Ljubljana registration plate and he waves.

Shit. Too late now. Anyway — she thinks, as the man takes hold of his suitcase and moves towards her — *it can't be him.*

Rebeka gets out of the car, says *breathe, girl*, and walks to the boot. The man puts down his suitcase and stares at the tall, tanned woman. Other than her olive skin, everything on her body was — from her hair, to her dress and large sunglasses — completely black.

'Can I get in the front?'

That's his voice. I recognise it from the very first time he said my name. 'Rebeka,' just like that, as he entered the classroom, 'wait here after class.'

'Of course.'

Will he notice my hands trembling on the wheel?

'Are you heading to Ljubljana too?' he asks after a minute of silence.

'Yes.'

'Were you camping here?'

'We've got a house here. Near Premantura.'

I hope my voice has changed enough after all these years. And that he keeps the chat to a minimum. Please let this be over.

'My wife and I have been going to this camp for eight years and we love it. Wouldn't change a thing. But I happened to have an appointment in Ljubljana tomorrow morning, and my wife said I should order one of these liftshares so she can keep the car.' He hesitates for a moment and says, 'That's... women for you.'

I don't remember him having a wife at the time. But we never actually spoke about it. Nothing else seemed to matter back then.

'What about you? Will you come back again?'

'Yeah, I've just got a couple of days at work to do. The husband and kids will be waiting for me, on the beach I expect.'

'What do you do? If it's not top secret.'

I remember the agonising hour of IT. He didn't even look at me. When the bell rang, and classmates jostled their way out of the classroom, he would close the door behind them and slowly make his way over to my desk. I wanted to shrink away behind that big computer. 'Rebeka,' he said, 'I think we need to talk.'

'C-Sure. Do you know it?'

'The Centre for Cybersecurity?'

'That's the one.'

'I know a bit about that world. I was an IT teacher for many years.'

I nod. He obviously doesn't recognise me. I breathe a sigh of relief. But there's still a long way to go before Ljubljana.

'So you're one of us then, are you?' he asks.

'Sort of. Though I actually trained as a criminologist.'

I remember how he leaned in towards me. 'I've had my eye on you for some time now, and I know that you're not paying the slightest bit of attention to my lessons.' He came right up close. I could smell the minty chewing gum on his breath. 'And last time you were here, you forgot to delete your search history.' I remember every single word as if it were yesterday.

Rebeka exits the motorway at Poreč.

'I've got one more person to pick up,' she says.

A guy in a Hawaiian shirt is waiting at a bus stop.

'Hi,' he says, opening the back door and getting in, 'Rebeka, isn't it,' and without waiting for a reply, he adds: 'How are we all doing?'

Please let this be over. It was so many years ago. And Rebeka is hardly an unusual name.

'Rebeka,' repeats the man in the passenger seat. 'Rebeka,' as if he were trying to remember something. And then he turns to face her. 'Rebeka? Is that you?'

My stomach flips. I'm transported back to that same feeling, hiding away at the back of the room and fearing what was about to happen next. 'And I was rather surprised by what I saw in your search history. And for such a good student. At least that's what everyone thinks.'

'Do you remember me? I was your IT teacher at school. Gosh — that must have been...'

'Fifteen years ago,' the woman says, removing her sunglasses.

We would normally meet up after that lesson, when the school was virtually empty. I was like an administrator for the school website, so we had a good alibi.

'You haven't changed,' he says, clearly flustered. His eyes wander over her figure. Small breasts, a dark, even suntan; greenish-grey eyes. 'Not one bit.'

And that, let me say, takes daily gym visits and a small fortune spent at the beautician. Whereas you, if I'm being honest, are barely recognisable.

'You barely recognise me, I know,' he says. 'Not all of us are blessed with such good genes.'

Rebeka says nothing, neither does he, and the guy in the back is glued to his phone.

He's waiting for me to say something, I imagine. But what am I supposed to say? Those years were completely out of control. Even now, I can't get my head around how I could be so stupid. Whilst the other girls were living their normal teenage lives, I was sneaking off to his classroom. I had no idea of the risk we were taking. But I was fifteen! And he was a grown-up. A teacher.

'It's fate,' he says. 'Fate is crazy, Rebeka. All these years and we've never bumped into one another. Not once. And now, here we are, sharing a lift! Not something people my age tend to do, either. And now the two of us meet here. In the middle of Istria, in the height of summer. After all these years.'

'That's mad, that is,' the guy in the back pipes up. 'It's

like something from that book, from those stories about lift sharing. What's it called again? *Good Company*, I think.'

Once he walked past me and a group of girlfriends in the corridor, just as we were giggling about something else. Later that afternoon, he said to me: 'Rebeka, you do know that we have to keep this between us?' 'I know. That's what we agreed.' I was a bag of nerves. But — of all the things I learnt during those years, it was IT that taught me the most. 'So what's interrupting your summer holidays?' the man turns to the guy in the back and smiles.

'I'm a dancer. Today's my first performance after being injured for five months. I can feel the adrenaline rising already.'

'Were you badly hurt?'

'I mean, I got through it, ha ha. I used the time to catch up with uni work. I actually fell from the stage and broke my leg. We'd just filmed this amazing video with PJ. But now,' he says, tapping his head, 'everything should be fine. My physiotherapist is a total sweetheart, that's all I'm saying.'

I can't say he ever forced me, though. 'Are you sure you want to do this?' he would ask. And: 'Do you realise what the consequences might be?' I always said yes. And, it's hard to admit this now, but during that time I really did relish the danger. I was hooked. And the money wasn't bad, either. But I don't think it was ever really about that. It was more about living on the edge...

'The whole crew were massively supportive for those five months, I have to say,' the guy continued, 'and I got used to it all, everything except the big cast on my leg. That was a laugh... especially when getting into cars.'

'You're better now, that's the main thing,' the man says.

'I saw quite a few accidents during my teaching years. Not a sports day went by without someone being taken to hospital. Proms were another hazard. But young people always pull through. It's how it is. And that's how it should be,' he says, and looks at the driver.

'Don't forget to drop me off at Koper,' the guy says.

'Shit, yeah,' Rebeka stammers and indicates. 'Sorry.'

One afternoon, the headmistress appeared out of nowhere in the IT classroom. 'Oh! Rebeka!' she exclaimed, staring in shock, 'I didn't know you were still in here.' I froze in fear. If she comes and looks at the screen... 'We're updating the news section on the website,' he said, with complete composure. 'Ah,' she replied, 'excellent work,' turning on her heels and squeezing her ample behind through the classroom door. It shook us both. After that we were more careful.

'Thanks, you're a diamond,' the guy says, as he gets his crutches together. 'Just here is great. Have a good day, *ciao*!' He's almost singing by the end, and he disappears.

For a while, they drive on in silence. Rebeka feels his eyes on her.

'So...' he hesitates, and then pauses. 'After that time... did you ever...?'

'No. Never,' Rebeka replies.

How could I have done? My career led me in a completely different direction.

'Did you?'

What am I going to do if he says yes? Am I going to be professionally, ethically obliged to do something?

'No, my dear Rebeka,' he says. 'Never again. Those years we shared were... wild. But it's not for me. These days I feel better on firmer, more legal ground.'

For a while he says nothing, and then exhales: 'I've never had as much money since, mind you. But I sleep soundly instead. And you can't put a price on that.'

'Course,' Rebeka says, and looks at him. 'Especially when, and I speak from experience, people aren't so naive these days. Whoever gets involved in that stuff now has to be ten times better prepared than we were.'

All of a sudden, she bursts out laughing.

'The Prince of Nigeria wishes to transfer the sum of 10,000 dollars. We must've been out of our minds.'

He looks at her, his best student. They drive in silence for a while.

'I don't suppose you fancy stopping for a drink, do you?'

THE TEN COMMANDMENTS

'The worst thing was,' he said, struggling with one hand to open a packet of chewing gum, 'that I'd replied straightaway and told her I'd be waiting by the taxi rank. Train station, taxi rank. She then rings me twice, saying "I'm here." "So am I," I tell her. "Silver Megane." "I can't see you." And so we go round in circles. "Are you at the taxi rank?" "Yeah, here by the entrance," she says. "Which entrance?" "By the McDonalds, I mean." "For the third time: I'm waiting for you by the taxi rank." Unbelievable. I had to wait a whole five minutes for the young woman to saunter over to the taxis. But listen to what she said next: "There are taxis over there by the entrance too, you know." I snapped. And who wouldn't have done? "By all means, take a taxi to Koper if there's a problem" I said. She glanced over at the other passenger, that nice-looking student, and rolled her eyes. I'd kick her out of the car if I could, but then it'd only be more hassle. I had a think about it, and then when I got home, I added a line to my usual terms and conditions: PLEASE FAMILIARISE YOURSELF WITH PICK UP LOCATION PRIOR TO DEPARTURE.'

With his left hand resting on the steering wheel, he managed to wrestle two chewing gums out of the packet and shove them into his mouth. 'How about that time I got the guy with dreads. They always seem dodgy to me, straight off. Are you gonna find a guy with dreads in a regular job? No, you won't. Are you gonna find a guy with dreads who isn't stoned? No, you won't. So, this young rasta sits in the front and the second we get on the motorway, he starts rolling a fag. Now, I know it was only tobacco because I'd got my eye on him. If he'd have pulled anything green out of his pocket, I swear the only place I'd be taking him would be the nearest police station. And as he rolls, he smooths it with his finger, up and down, up and down, and then — I knew exactly what was coming — he asks if we can stop for a fag break. I politely decline; he can smoke at home, the cheeky son of a bitch. He ruined my whole day. That evening, when I'd come round a bit, I added the following line to my document: NO FAG BREAKS, NO DRUG USERS.'

He then skipped between radio stations for a while. He didn't stick with a single hit and would never listen to more than three or four seconds before changing stations. 'It's all bollocks. It's all a load of bollocks. Now we've got YouTube, the only thing radio's good for is the shops. Radio 1, Val 202, and those classical ones — they should get rid of all that state bullshit in one fell swoop. Be ruthless,' he said, turning it off.

'The worst one was that bird in a tracksuit that I picked up like, where was it again? At Kino Šiška, maybe. Anyway, she turns up in a tracksuit. How do people not get this? A tracksuit's for cleaning your gaff, you can't go out in public like that. These people have turned Ljubljana into a fairground, to put it politely. On the journey back it got worse. These two dizzy blondes from Portorož turn up. They can't have been much older than 20. They'd gone to the beach for the day, they said, and wouldn't stop laughing about something. It didn't take me long to get wind of them. Literally. One of them burped and the other started giggling so much that I thought I was going to have to stop the car. I turned the AC up on full, hoping to make a point, but nothing. And then — Andrej, listen to this — out of nowhere, one of them says: "Do you mind if I take my shoes off?" I said nothing. "These blisters are proper killing me." And they burst out laughing again. But what could I do, she went ahead and took her shoes off. First her trainers, and then her socks as well! And she carefully places them on the middle seat. These small, white cotton socks. I wanted to throw up. They did not smell like the feet of a twenty-year-old girl: more like those of a crusty, fungal old man. It nearly finished me off. As soon as I'd tipped them out in Ljubljana, I took myself straight to the car wash. Later, of course, I had to write: I DON'T TAKE DRUNKS. SHOES MUST NOT BE REMOVED INSIDE THE VEHICLE.'

He took an old receipt out of the door compartment, straightened it out and wrapped his chewing gum inside. He dropped the scrunched-up ball back in the compartment and gave a heavy sigh. 'Things quietened down for a while after that... but I remember this one day clearly: July, baking hot, and some guy gets in. About my age, I'd say. Looked tidy, was on time... I must say, he seemed very friendly, and so I started asking him a few questions about what he did. He said he writes this blog, WakeUpSlovenia. And then he went on a bit about how we shouldn't believe everything we're told. I couldn't agree more with him on that. And then when I said that as far as I'm concerned, they could get rid of the state broadcasters tomorrow and that all those commies sitting comfy up there ought to be out picking potatoes, well, this really got him going. "Have you ever wondered how much autism was around when we were younger?" he asked, almost trembling he was so worked up. "Have you ever wondered why doctors never provide evidence of side effects from vaccinations? Have you ever wondered when it became a crime to think for yourself?" Well, I had to stop him there for a moment. "My ex worked at Lek," I said, "so I know a fair bit about this sort of thing, and vaccines are one of those, well, necessary evils. It's the best we've got." Then he started giving me loads of shit about increasingly crackpot theories, before eventually saying: "Anyway, you can take a look at the interview with Norma Korošec, who's done extensive research into it all. You'll find a link on my blog, WakeUpSlovenia." "You have to bring her up, of all people." "She's a strong woman," he said. Luckily, we then arrived at Oli Burger, where he got out. My head was throbbing. These are the kind of guys whose unvaccinated kids are infecting our nurseries, and then at home they're wanking over Norma Korošec. I was fuming. I immediately added: ANTI-VAXXERS ARE NOT WELCOME.'

'But I'm telling you, Andrej,' he continued, after some reflection, 'the worst time was this thirsty bunch of students. We hadn't even got onto the motorway and they were getting their water bottles out of their rucksacks and chugging it down. As if they were bloody house plants. As if they couldn't have a nice, pleasant glass of water at home. No; students today only chug. And if they can do anything about it, it's only from those eco-bottles. If they've got themselves a bottle of water from the kiosk, I keep schtum. But I can't stand the sight of those eco-bottles. They cost at least 20 euros. And then it's all "poor students" who can't afford a car. And they rely on us. Gross. I've lost my rag over this so many times, that one day I wrote: FOOD AND DRINK ARE NOT TO BE CONSUMED INSIDE THE VEHICLE (INCLUDING WATER).'

'I thought that was the end of it and that I was safe,' he said, and keeping his left hand on the wheel, he made another awkward reach to get a CD from the dashboard. He eventually managed to stick an album of Dalmatian classics into the player. 'Not yet, my friend. This one time, a young girl turns up, with the tips of her hair dyed blue — so you know straightaway that she's not quite right. "I was hoping I'd get to meet you, actually," she says to me, somewhere en route. "You've got such a sense of humour." "Excuse me?" "These terms of yours. On your profile, I mean. A critique of modern-day society in a nutshell. Bravo." I wasn't quite sure what to make of that, but I chose not to encourage further conversation. It's like I said: she's got blue hair, she's not all there. Sat next to her was some dude — a young guy in a jacket. He said he was going to his brother's graduation ball. And then the traffic was obviously bad on Šmartinka, and the guy was getting more and more twitchy, sitting there sweating like a pig in this dark blue shirt. When we finally make it out of the jam, he says: "Would you mind taking me straight to the Exhibition Hall, please? I'm already late as it is, and if I have to wait for the bus too…" I said nothing. What does this kid think I am? A taxi service? "I can pay extra," he said. He looked in his wallet. "I've got twenty euros in cash; you can have it all." I took him into town; twenty euros extra is better than a slap in the face. But still, the arrogance of this kid got my back up. Which is why, the following day, I added: RIDES ARE ONLY, AND EXCLUSIVELY, TO THE AGREED DROP-OFF LOCATION. And that afternoon, I added this in brackets, too: (EVEN IN THE CASE OF DELAYS).'

With one hand, he rummaged in the glove compartment and swerved dangerously to the right. He eventually located his sunglasses and put them on. 'That's right, Andrej,' he sighed. "There's all kinds of strange folk in this world. And the saddest thing is, is that you seem to get more and more of them. Recently I got a request for a ride from some guy, this Mirko, who asked me to pick him up from the bus stop next to Metelkova. That in itself was suspicious. I avoid Metelkova like the plague. He then mentioned that he was on crutches and it would be difficult for him to meet me at the station. It was right after the Christmas holidays, so I immediately put two and two together. First he pisses about on skis in Switzerland, and then whinges when he breaks a bone. I know the sort. No accountability whatsoever. I said I was already fully booked, even though he probably sussed that it was an easy excuse. I really didn't care. I wrote: WILL ONLY PICK UP FROM THE TRAIN STATION (NO EXCEPTIONS). A man has to have clear boundaries. If you don't establish order straightaway…'

'By the way, speaking of crutches — I've just remembered this one infamous trip. The first and last time that I drove any gays. Two of them, sat on the back seat: one looking like a model, with his eyebrows pencilled in no doubt; and the other, who looked like he hadn't set foot in a gym for years. Anyway, these two gays sit in the back, holding hands now and again. Now I don't have anything against their sort, don't get me wrong — but that sort of thing should be kept safely behind closed doors. You know what I mean… I'll say no more. Anyway, we're driving along and the conversation turns to disabled people. To parking spaces for the disabled. The chubby one says: "I think it's shameful how people park in designated spaces." He said it just like that. That's how gay people talk. "Totally. There's no excuse for it," says the model. "But have either of you ever wondered," I interrupt, because I couldn't keep quiet, "why there's a million disabled spaces outside every damn shop?" I paused, for dramatic effect. "Why are there ten, twelve disabled spaces in front of Baumax or Obi? Do disabled people really flock to buy handsaws? Or tiles; do they go get them at Merkur and spend the weekend tiling at home? No. Has anyone ever seen a disabled person trimming a hedge? No. I mean, with all due respect. I don't have anything against them, don't get me wrong. But we've got to be able to say what's what. It's a conspiracy between businesses and the police, so they can dole out parking tickets and line their pockets. And the little guy gets screwed. It's an open secret. A guy can nip out for three minutes, he's just come to get a boiler filter, but the car park's full, and he's got to pick his kid up from school, the little guy, who just wants to get on with his own life, then gets a ticket from the police, just because he's parked in some disabled space. The height of stupidity, if you ask me." And that's what I told them. Properly got it off my chest. I'm not sure what they made of it though; the gays kept quiet all the way to Koper. And this is what was bothering me the next day… I wanted to write: sorry, no homosexuals, but I know that I'd have the LGBT lobby on my back straightaway. All those fat, angry feminists. They can properly come down on you, that lot. But it was also like I

228

said: I've got nothing against gays. So I gave it some thought and wrote: PHYSICAL CONTACT INSIDE THE VEHICLE IS PROHIBITED.'

The final track of the CD was coming to an end. The songwriters had lavished praise on women, the ocean, seagulls and Dalmatian islands. 'But the worst one was a month or so ago. Some guy gets in, full of himself, saying that he's off on holiday. And then he starts explaining how this last time he took a ride, he was in a car with a mixed-race woman. And that she was good looking, but a bit strange. And he starts going on about how he doesn't have anything against black people, but that he doesn't think it's right to mix races. "Our bodies are built to live in Europe. We're not Eskimos, who can be surrounded by snow the whole year round; and we're not black people either, who can withstand non-stop 40-degree sunshine beating down on them. It's called evolutionary adaptation. So you can't, I don't know, plant a pine tree in the desert. Or in Antarctica. It's the same with races. But don't ever say that out loud, whatever you do. Because we're all so politically correct." There was a girl in the car at the time, who said that her grandma was from northern Germany, and thanks to her dad's side she was part Serbian and part Hungarian, so what did he think about that? "If my ancestors had never mixed, I wouldn't exist at all," she said, with a tremble in her voice. "Ah, you see that's okay," the guy says. "Those are all Europeans; that's all our European culture." "Oh I see," said the girl, "so it's breeding with — hang on — black people, Chinese people and Eskimos that's the issue, if I've got that right." "No need to get worked up about it," the guy says. The whole journey, ruined. I'm telling you, these right-wingers know how to kill the mood. They're just like those crusaders, of course, who want a white, Christian Europe, yet they can't get it into their thick-as-shit heads that they're using Arabic numerals. And, I was thinking about this, we've got to make it clear what we think of their politics. There's no place for them in the twenty-first century. I wrote down: THIS VEHICLE WELCOMES LIBERAL, OPEN-MINDED PEOPLE.'

'What happened last week, though, was — how shall I put this, Andrej — the straw that broke the camel's back. This bird rings up, saying — I've forgotten her name — that she'd like to book a lift to Koper. She was so well-spoken that I assumed this was some important person, so I was happy at first, and agreed to the lift. Then she was asking something, some little detail about whether I stop at the services if necessary, and if someone were cold would I turn up the heating, and if I allow drinking water to be consumed in the car in the case of long delays. "Look," I said, "anything can be arranged. We're all human, aren't we?" "Fine," she said. "Just one more thing," she said, "I'm calling from TV Slovenija, from the *On Our Roads* programme. We're putting together a piece about lift sharing and we'd like to invite you to take part." "Why me?" "Well… a few passengers have got in touch with us, Mr Andrej… to do with your, how shall I call them, extensive rules." "What is this, some sort of secret camera?" "No," she said, reciting her name and repeating why they would like to film me. A darkness descended over my eyes. "I cannot consent to that," I said. "And the lift is now cancelled." Then I hung up and my day was ruined. Journalists really are the dregs of humanity. The worst of the worst. But those communist arseholes from TV Slovenija are the worst of all. As if some brat reporter is going to harass me like that. I opened my laptop and added: JOURNALISTS ARE NOT WELCOME IN THIS VEHICLE.' He once again fumbled awkwardly with his right hand for the packet of chewing gum and eventually teased out the last two pieces and shoved them in his mouth. 'And then the next morning, it dawned on me. I don't need any of this. I give lifts to all kinds of weird and troublesome people; I lose sleep over them, I write guidelines, I behave properly, I'm fair; and this is what I get thrown in my face. Total, utter ingratitude. "No," I said to myself, "you really don't need any of this, Andrej." And I went over to my computer and turned it on, and then for one final time opened that godforsaken website with its little orange camel in the top left-hand corner and deleted my profile. And now,' he said, laughing out loud, 'I drive solely and exclusively in good company.'

HOW DOES A CAT FEEL
WHEN STROKED?

'That'll be fine, of course it's fine,' I said.

She spoke in such an elusive, roundabout way that even the soothing tone of her voice wasn't enough to keep me from checking the time.

'And you're sure that you don't discriminate against… how should I put this… certain physical conditions?'

'No, not in the slightest. But like I said, there's no space for a wheelchair, because I've got my daughter's bed frame in the boot.'

'There won't be a wheelchair. I'd rather not go into detail about my physical condition just now, but I can guarantee that I won't take up any more space than a regular passenger.'

'So we're settled, then. I'll be waiting by the old steam train in front of the station, is that ok?'

'Of course, I'll be there. You'll recognise my voice.'

***

Sunday dinner was tense again. My wife and I just haven't known what to do these past few months. 'It's alright for you; at least you don't have to see it during the week,' she said, before turning out the light, 'it can get to Friday and she won't have said a single word.' Feeling helpless, I said nothing. My wife has responded to this new, unknown sense of powerlessness with anger. 'My evenings will be spent looking at her miserable face and I won't get a peep out of her.'

The worst thing is that we don't know what we've done wrong. Our daughter just slowly stopped speaking to us. She glides around the house like a ghost. My wife's most recent idea was that her bedroom was dripping in negative energy, and so we moved her into the bigger room in the attic, bought her new furniture and arranged it according to some hippy-dippy principle about eliminating sharp corners. The cost alone ought to have triggered an avalanche of words to come tumbling out of her mouth — yet still she said nothing. At first we thought it was her way of dealing with my absence — I'm only at home on the weekends. But when I was offered a job in the capital, I had a long conversation with our daughter (back when she was still normal). She insisted on multiple occasions that it 'wasn't a big deal'. Before adding, finally: 'Dad, it's not like I've got free time in the week anyway.'

I could hear she was in the bathroom. 'I'm going to say goodbye,' I mumbled to my wife, wrapping my robe around me.

I knocked twice, opened the door and leant against the doorframe. She was standing at the sink, cleansing her face with some cotton wool. She kept her back to me but looked at me through the mirror. I opened my arms out wide and stood up straight (once we'd tried everything else, my wife and I had gone to a body language workshop). 'Hey,' I began, as if I felt awkward talking to my own daughter. She looked at me and carried on wiping her forehead with a piece of cotton wool. 'I heard you were in here, so I came to say goodnight. I'm off tomorrow, probably before you wake up.' She looked at me, and all I saw, if anything at all, was the dejection in her eyes. Or was that just another word for emptiness?

***

The next morning, as I waited at the traffic lights, I texted a passenger to say that I was going to be late, though as it happened the traffic quickly cleared, which meant that I arrived at the station only a couple of minutes later than we'd agreed. Walking towards me was a guy with a suitcase, which I fitted into the boot amongst the bits of bed, and a girl with a large black bag, which she clutched to her body the entire time. They sat in the back. The ones who go for the back seat never start conversations, which I was thankful for on this occasion. 'We're just waiting for one more girl,' I said, breaking the silence. All I heard from the back was an ambivalent 'Mhm'. I'm always happy to wait a few minutes for latecomers and there's no way I want to be one of those uptight drivers who ring and pester straightaway. Yet after five minutes of silence with no sign of the third passenger, I gave her a call.

'Oh hi there, just wondering if you were nearly here?'

'Yes, I'm here.'

'Where?'

'Here, by the steam train.'

'I'm here too, in the grey Volvo.'

'Yes, I see you.'

'Come over, we're already running late.'

'I'm standing right by the car — could you please open the door?'

Ohhh… it dawned on me, finally. She's a dwarf. That's why she was asking about… ah, ok. I got out and walked around the car. There was nobody there. But all of a sudden, she spoke.

'Here I am.'

I turned around, once again looking down… I couldn't see anyone, anywhere.

'I'm standing right next to you,' she said. The voice really was very close.

'Where are you? I can't see anyone. What are you?' The hairs on the back of my neck started crawling. If this is some sort of sick joke or hidden camera, they can pack it in. What sort of prank is this?

'You can't see me, but I am here, next to you. Open the door for me, please.'

'What?'

Someone walked past and stared. And why wouldn't they — there's a man in the pickup zone, talking to himself. The passengers in the back were eyeing me suspiciously, too.

'How? Why can't I see you? Who are you?'

'It's like I told you: my physical condition is… a little unusual. You did say you were okay with that. You said you didn't discriminate.'

I stared into the space ahead of me. The voice was a metre or so away, at a guess. I then slowly approached the spot where I'd pinpointed the voice and opened the door.

'Thank you,' she said.

'May I close it?'

'Yes, thank you.'

I went back to the driver's door and tentatively got in the car. What do I do? Nothing, I said to myself. Just get to work.

I didn't say a word. I can't see straight. First it came for my daughter, and now it's come for me. It's just like in *Blindness*, only sight isn't the only thing we're losing. The passengers in the back sat there, rigid. I'm sure I wasn't the only one who just wanted this journey to be over as quickly and safely as possible.

'Apologies,' I said to them. A muffled 'Mhm' was all that came from the back.

'No worries,' said the voice from the passenger seat, 'It's not exactly typical. I completely understand your reaction.' Everything was still for a moment. I thought I heard a quiet sigh to my right. 'Maybe I should be the one to apologise to you, for giving you a fright.'

I forced my eyes to remain fixed on the road, but through the corner of my eye snatched a glance at the air beside me.

'You don't have anything to apologise for,' I heard myself saying. The passengers in the back had forgotten to close their mouths. 'You haven't done anything wrong; I just didn't expect you to be…'

'To be invisible,' she said, finishing my sentence.

'But why? I mean, this is impossible.'

'I used to think so too. And then one day, late into my childhood, I just — started to disappear. At first people said I looked pale. Then sickly. Then they said I was barely visible. Then etheric. And then, well, one morning, I went into the kitchen and nobody noticed me. I sat down on the sofa, said something, and nearly gave my grandma a heart attack.'

'And what happened then?'

'Well, in actual fact, nothing really changed. I dropped out of school, which was for the best, and I focused on what I love doing the most. I love listening to music and stroking the cat.'

'But what about... what happened to your body?'

'I can still feel it. Right now, for example, I've got an itch just above my ear and I scratched it. I can move things, too. I can turn pages. I can turn on the tap and feel water on my hands. I can actually open car doors for myself too, but that would only have frightened you even more. And, if I'm honest, I'm fond of a gentleman,' she said, giggling. Her laugh was pure; almost childlike, but a little flirtatious at the same time.

'But why did this happen to you?'

'I don't know, to be honest. As you can imagine, I'm rather... how should I put it... unique. I do have a hunch about what caused it, though. As to why I started to disappear. And, if I think back, the reason's actually quite boring. Trivial. It was a harsh and unjust form of punishment. But how do you explain that to your thirteen-year-old self?'

I said nothing. I was hoping she would continue. I got the sense that I was starting to catch on, though to what exactly, I wasn't yet sure.

'You know, I was a really cute kid. The most beautiful girl in my class. But I was also incredibly shy, and more importantly, incredibly sensitive. And everyone around me mistook that sensitivity for arrogance. My teacher, schoolfriends, neighbours. That nonsense then ultimately infiltrated my parents' psyche. I felt it keenly, not that they mentioned anything at first. I could feel they were unhappy with me. They thought they had a stuck-up daughter, and they were grappling with it inside. They couldn't understand why I didn't want to play with schoolfriends who squashed ants under their shoes, putting them in jars for pickling. Or why I preferred to stay in my room, listening to music and stroking the cat. They couldn't understand why I didn't want to leave the flat if I could hear neighbours in the hallway. They thought it was arrogant and antisocial, but I had actually been avoiding the neighbours ever since they'd asked me who I liked the most: mummy or daddy. And then one day, at lunchtime, Mum lost her temper with me: 'What good are those golden curls and that pretty face of yours, if there's nothing behind those dark eyes?' And Dad added: 'In the end, it's brains, not beauty, that count.'

She paused for a while. I could have sworn I felt her turn and gaze out of the window.

'I reckon that was the moment in which I began to disappear.'

'You know what, I think I've read something like this somewhere before.'

'Yeah, you'll have read it in *The Moomins*. I wrestled with this a lot at first; whether I'd brought in on myself, because back then I read *The Moomins* a lot, almost obsessively. Maybe some scary, self-fulfilling prophecy had descended upon me. Yet slowly I began to discover that being invisible really wasn't that scary. That invisibility was my preferred state of being.'

She paused once again.

'And I sorted out my shyness, too. Just look at how openly I'm sharing things with you. I realised that I actually love talking. With those who listen to me, of course. And by some twist of fate, the only ones who listen are those I like to talk to. Others can't bring themselves to talk to me — they're paralysed by their fear of the invisible. So I've become a real chatterbox recently. As you've probably noticed.'

'I don't know about that. You seem like a very pleasant person to talk to.'

'Thank you. Is there anything you'd like to talk about with me?'

For a while I didn't say anything, even though for a few minutes I had known what the feeling was; what I had begun to feel earlier was an understanding.

'Actually, there is something I'd like to talk to you about. My daughter has stopped talking to me and my wife. She's stopped talking. She just looks at us. Sometimes I think that she's looking at us with disappointment; sometimes with exhaustion, but mostly without any will to live. As if... as if she just doesn't feel anything anymore. As if there were no point in anything. You can imagine how desperate we are. But you have... how shall I put this... you've given me an idea.'

'I think I know what you're going to ask me, and I can tell you straightaway: it would be my pleasure.'

'How did you know?'

'Oh, come on. You desperate parents are so predictable,' she laughed. But it wasn't a mocking, or mean laugh; it was gentle, understanding, and soft.

***

As we approached the centre of town on the ring road, I first dropped off the young guy, and then the woman, who had been sat in the back.

'Those two will never speak a word of this to anyone. They'll be too frightened of people thinking they're insane,' she said.

'Can I ask you one more thing?'

'Of course.'

'Can a cat feel your hands on its back?'

'That I don't know, as I'm not a cat. But I do know that they always purr.'

I parked at the stop, opened the door for her and waited a few moments.

'Goodbye. See you again,' I said.

She laughed. 'That's unlikely, but we'll be in touch about the visit. I look forward to meeting your daughter,' she said, before saying goodbye.

I got back in the car and took a deep breath. I then placed a hand on the car seat, where she had been sat. It was warm.

SONJA ŽIVALJEVIĆ

Montenegro

Sonja Živaljević's nine fragments titled 'Metohija: Tapestry Without a Frame' portray multicultural life in the Serbian Autonomous Province of Kosovo (now the Republic of Kosovo) before the breakup of Yugoslavia in the 1990s. Ethnic Albanians, Turks, Serbs and Montenegrins mingle. These autobiographical pieces, which centre around the author's early struggle with tuberculosis, are written in a calm, melancholic style with startling imagery and many historical and literary references — a veritable kaleidoscope of the Balkans. Women's prose in Montenegro does not have a long tradition and is a relatively marginal phenomenon. Živaljević herself is above all a poet, editor and non-fiction writer, having only ventured into prose in recent years. This could explain the clear poetic licence of her pieces in this book. Women writers in Montenegro today tend to deal with the position of Montenegrin women in history or with amorous themes, Živaljević says, and some are feministically oriented or inclined towards other forms of social activism. She, on the other hand, draws inspiration mainly from folk literature with its sense of beauty, legends and links to nature.

Metohija:[2] Tapestry Without a Frame:

Turkish coffee

Aunty Trasha watched us from her bed, curled up like a black cat with a paw under its head. The lighting in the women's ward of the Hospital for Pulmonary Diseases was soft and gentle, and at dusk, when there were no more doctors, visitors or nurses, it felt as if we indulged in the soothing, rounded contours of our white beds and the new hues of the pale-green walls. And the silence that, like a paper towel, quickly absorbed everything: the city outside, the corridors, and time itself.

Beautiful Meliha, from a Turkish family, with a fine complexion and long, thin fingers, got up to make coffee. For the last time. She was to be discharged and would continue her treatment at home, but the prospect brought no joy or change to her face. The shadow that fell over half her forehead and one of her deep, dark eyes like the end of a kerchief, even when she smiled at my childish antics, didn't go away.

She said this was the only way to make Turkish coffee.

---

2 A historical region of Serbia, now the southwestern part of Kosovo.

She'd devote herself completely to the ritual, every time, and in the winter twilight all her movements — measured, slow and elegant — looked like the dance of an Oriental Princess, a small performance for Trasha and me alone to enjoy. When all the accessories had emerged from her bedside table and stood ready, and had been inspected and cleaned if she deemed it necessary, she poured sugar and coffee into a ceramic cup, slowly added water and put the cup on a small portable stove. She took the silver spoon and gently stirred the magical beverage, whose scent spread through our room, wound around like dark silk embroidered with gold thread, and descended onto Persian carpets, which soared into the sky and carried Aunty Trasha, Meliha and me far, far away.

***

I was seventeen. It was the beginning of an unusually hot September in 1980 when I was first brushed by the feather, the one whose touch suddenly makes the whole world become perfect, candyflossy, and your legs stop obeying your head because a new wind rises in it. Especially when the young man in question is leaving for the big city to study, and your heart doesn't know what to do in the situation. It just sways like a balloon whose string can slip out of your hand any minute. It could not be helped — he went away to study, and soon afterward I was admitted to the pulmonary ward. Without a word of warning, tuberculosis tied the balloon firmly to the bar of an iron hospital bed. With a double knot and no bow.

That fall from celestial heights, from love and hope, into a hospital bed, whose iron frame was always icy cold, however hot the consumptive hand was which touched it, brought not only acute pain — but complete disintegration.

I seemed to sleep without end in the first few weeks in hospital. Every morning, the nurse would put out twelve little tablets for me. I always left the multivitamin tablet, the only pink and sweet one, like a lolly, until last. Then I'd be given an injection (I didn't know I'd been prescribed a total of ninety) and sank into a feverish stupor, dark green with smears of petroleum, which you can't thrash your way out of, and my skinny limbs squeezed and convulsed to help in the battle raging throughout my body. Not only in my lungs.

When the mist began to rise from the battlefield, when my head cleared a little, I asked to be brought books from home — one volume at a time of Fyodor Dostoyevsky, from the set with blue covers. I immersed myself to find a cold stone for my boiling forehead, a dry pathway for longer breath, which led into a sea of questions and dilemmas, into new labyrinths and darkness, to the depths, where the most light came from. It was faint, almost an illusion, but still light.

***

'It's not good for your eyes to read so much. You're young and should take care of your eyes,' Aunty Trasha would say. So, together, we took care of my eyes by talking. About everything, because women always have things to talk about, softly, taking care not to tire ourselves out. Sometimes with long breaks. Occasionally Trasha would drift off in the middle of a sentence. I never knew if she was just pausing, or sleeping, so I'd stay quiet and rest until she spoke again — and continued exactly where she'd left off.

I fell in love with her immediately, the day she came. Black and white, with a little red. Everything on her was immaculately clean and starched. A snow-white shirt, black apron, short black vest and embroidered socks were all part of the Albanian costume, perhaps taken out of her dowry box for the first time. Trasha slept in a long white nightshirt. I saw it, as well as her fine silver chain with a cross, although she always undressed in the dark when she thought no one could see her. She lived in the same village where she'd been born, not far from Đakovo (Gjakova in Albanian).

She was in hospital for the first time in her life. She didn't have tuberculosis, she assured me, but some other disease, so they put her here until they worked out what it was — in a room with infectious cases. Brilliant, I thought. True, she didn't have a cough, and she wasn't pale or unhealthily red. Her therapy consisted of two or three tablets. She seemed healthy, just very, very tired. She took an interest in stories about my childhood, school and my heartthrob, and she'd liven up, ask me things, and I was able to make her laugh. So I'd happily go on describing events and telling her jokes and anecdotes. I, in turn, was fascinated by everything to do with her village and her life, so similar to that of my kind and shrewd grandmother.

***

I couldn't work out Trasha's age — maybe she was about seventy. Meliha was twenty-five and had two children. She cared more about them than herself. She made sure I didn't notice that she took care of me like a child, so it wouldn't offend me. I was no longer a child. I read Dostoyevsky, and I thought about all kinds of things: about death, and the danger that I could infect another person, and that maybe no one would love me because I'd always be skinny, bony and sickly, and that maybe I wouldn't have children. If I got better at all. I was a 'serious case'.

Meliha spoke softly, as if to herself, so we didn't always understand her well, although she spoke excellent Serbian, like Trasha. She was deeply and devotedly silent, like now when she held the cup with both hands and stared at what we couldn't see. One quickly gets used to such people — to their consideration, gentle attention and even their absence and silence. I admired her beauty and natural elegance. A degree of distance was thus appropriate, but sometimes I'd jump onto her bed and touch her shoulder or arm; I don't know why, I guess I wanted to inhale the scent of a mother.

Trasha explained to me that Meliha was pining because her family had decided to leave and move to Turkey. She had grown up in Peć (Peja) and loved the city, which didn't surprise me because everyone who grows up there loves it forever. The family was leaving because of the political situation — bad things were happening in Kosovo and they didn't want to take any risks.

Blossom

I took my first steps in paradise. It's a shame I don't remember. But maybe it's good I also don't remember our first departure, the move from there.

My brothers and I once went to see if our first home still existed.

During the reconstruction of Yugoslavia after the Second World War, attention was given to the development of fruit-growing. Metohija was ideally suited for this. A nursery existed between Dečani (Deçan) and Đakovo, and it was there that my father got his first job and brought his beautiful young wife with her long black plaits.

The nursery had since grown into a large, well-established orchard. The low, spartan red-roofed house, which had served both as offices and accommodation for young agronomists, now slumbered, a little dilapidated but content. It seemed to be enjoying the spring sunshine in the sea of blossom. In front of the entrance — a row of tall lilacs. Their branches swayed gently, heavy with clusters of purple flowers. Immediately behind them was a stone well with a rusty chain and no bucket. Chamomile and dandelion spread in concentric circles from the well into the distance, through the long rows of trees with their fluffy white hats, without end. The image shimmered in the merry, skittish breeze, which played in the petals, the hair on my forehead and the tufted clouds in the freshly painted sky.

We stood and watched for a long time, inhaling the scent of lilac.

Behind the house stood a crooked old apple tree with a single branch, leaning against the window frame with a broken pane. I shivered. Was it possible that I remembered only that: the tapping of the branch on the window pane? Fear? No, the tree was simply outside; it was cold and wanted to shelter from the wind, to come in and warm itself, for someone to hug it.

Who knows what that old tree and its tapping crafted inside us...

Before leaving, I stroked that single branch of my apple tree.

BLUE AND VIOLET

The new settlement at the entrance to Đakovo consisted of a double row of huts, each containing two flats. Between the huts and around them was a playground, a large meadow on the left, and a grove on the right, through which the women sometimes went to the spring, or down to the little river to bathe in the summer.

Colours are the first thing I can distinctly remember. Me, alone in the meadow, barefoot, a little cold, but holding a tiny blue flower. I was thrilled by that little thing, that sky I could touch.

And then in the grove, while trotting along after my mother, I slipped and fell off the path. I was lying on my tummy, my knees and elbows hurt a little, but I opened my eyes and saw a clump of violets right there and laughing at my nose. What a joy! I forgot my scratches and everything, I was happy and laughed together with those pale-purple stars that shone just for me amid the mouldy leaves.

Roses soon flourished along the path to our flat. I was intrigued to observe those conceited, thorny ladies from below. Red, yellow and white buds later bloomed like heads of lettuce and bent towards the ground on thin branches that could barely support them.

Aunty Olga often invited all the children from the huts, and there were many of us, to drop in for doughnuts. And radishes from the garden, which there were lots of, although Aunty Olga didn't have children of her own.

Calling us together was easy because we were constantly outside and played until dark. We thought up new games when the usual ones bored us: we split into two camps and fought battles, or chased after a ball, and even without a ball we ran, ran, ran...

We loved being together. One very snowy winter, I took a little bucket and started digging a tunnel to see my friend Marina across the way. I was so tenacious that, in the end, everyone grabbed shovels and dug paths between the huts. There were no more obstacles to seeing the neighbours.

I also loved Branko, the boy next door. He was a little older and much more serious, so much so that he didn't notice my wistful looks. He had buck teeth with a gap between them, which for some reason I found especially cute.

All sorts of things happened in those preschool years. Funny things, like the time my mother wanted to cook eel for lunch; she started screaming when the eel realised what was in store for it and slithered right out of the sink and out of the kitchen.

And little adventures, like when one of my brothers took me to the city to see a real bear. Tied with a thick chain, it obeyed its master, a Gypsy with a crumpled hat who never stopped talking. And the bear danced, it really did. I mean, it turned in a circle. I was fortunate to be able to watch everything from the safe height of my brother's shoulders.

And also things that angered me, like the time my brothers used my favourite doll as a model for a plaster mould. Or whenever they treated me not as a younger sister, but as a baby. And I'd always been big!

So many things… until the day of the move came. I'd turned seven and was about to start school — in Peć, where Dad had a new job.

The truck was ready. We were all ready. We wore our best for the trip, and I was in a light-coloured dress. I'd said goodbye to all the children. And to Aunty Olga. And Branko. With my favourite rubber tiger in my hand. The sun had risen but only warmed faintly, probably due to weariness, as was usual at the end of August. I stood there and tried once again to absorb everything, memorise everything. Hoping I'd never be forgotten by the meadow with the tiny blue flowers, the huts with two families in each and the grove with the violets. Nor by you, rose ladies.

Then blood started dripping from my nose. I stood, unable to move, while everyone jumped up. *Raise your arm! Tilt back your head! Don't worry about your dress, we have to go.*

I raised my arm and didn't worry about my dress. I didn't cry. We set off. I just stared at the roses, which were now all alone.

THE RAILWAY TRACK

Peć was the last station on the line, but the track continued on past the station, until the very end. That last section never saw any carriages, but it was a proper stretch of track with crushed stone and wooden sleepers that smelt of tar. We used to go along it to school, so it did play a significant role. Although we discovered the purpose of its existence in it being the shortest route, and great fun because we trained our balance by walking along the rails and kept fit by jumping from sleeper to sleeper, its abrupt end was a big puzzle.

It's probably the same at all terminal stations. There was nothing at the end of the track, although, logically, there should have been something — a buffer stop or a sign, a greeting, anything. Instead, the rails were cut off as if with a knife at a street that ran perpendicularly towards the city centre and ultimately stopped there. But it seemed to us that those two parallel lines continued their endless mission: the stupid asphalt street had rendered them invisible, yet they travelled on through sky and space, far and ever farther, like two parallel beams of light. We imagined that the stars hopped along on them, or they served as slides for fairies or other unseen creatures.

That's how I tried to explain the enigma. The end of the track troubled me later, too, when I started off along the asphalt in the other direction, towards the city centre and the lyceum. It aroused a vague sadness in me. And vague sorrows can last.

KING AND SAINT

The smell of roasted chestnuts wafted from the hallway and mingled with the smell of Meliha's coffee. Our half-glazed door was always open at that time. All three of us agreed: chestnuts grew along both roads to Dečani, from Peć and from Đakovo, but the ones that grew around the monastery itself were the sweetest in the whole world.

We often went to Dečani. Not always to the famous monastery from the fourteenth century, because my father, as a member of the Communist Party, was far from religious. But a minimum of tradition was maintained in our house. We dyed eggs for Easter, for example. No one tried to explain Christian symbolism, and children weren't interested. In the spring, when our spirits rose because everything was starting to bloom, one Sunday morning was especially bright, cheerful and filled with love: we played the egg-tapping game, eggs were given to other children in the neighbourhood, and families visited each other.

Easter was a sign that the time had come for weekends out of town.

***

Picnicking in the chestnut forest near Dečani was one of our favourite excursions. After a walk in the forest, we'd drink our fill of the excellent water in the monastery courtyard and breathe the fine air from Prokletije — the Accursed Mountains — which brought the freshness of the remaining snow. King Stefan must have been very special, I thought. What a brilliant place to choose for a monastery.

There's something about Dečani that isn't found anywhere else in the world. Maybe God sat down here for a rest, weary after creating the world. He leaned his back against Prokletije to get his breath back, to refresh himself with the scent of spruce and pine and water from the clear River Bistrica. And then, as his eyelids grew heavier and heavier, he looked out across the fertile plain of Metohija and the flat field of Kosovo as if in the tender shade of two rambler roses, and he saw less and less of that soothing window with its myriad colours and hues, and heard more and more of the sweet evening birdsong that heralds the coming of a sunny, flowery, perfect May day.

The church looked like something straight out of a fairy tale. Marble, delicate bands of colour, with a beautiful portal, high windows and strange stone heads. I especially liked the ornamental bands around the top of the church that resembled zigzagging lace on the hem of a skirt or fluttering from a sleeve.

My mother once took me to the monastery for a special reason. She tugged me by the hand because I kept stopping, enchanted by the warm colours, the light, the pleasant smell and a mysterious murmur, though I wasn't sure it really existed because I couldn't tell where it came from. I knew nothing about God, Christ or the saints. But it was lovely there. Enchanting.

We stood near Stefan Dečanski's coffin cum reliquary, which was raised off the floor just so much that a child could crawl through underneath. 'Go on,' my mother whispered, 'no one will mind, and it's good for your health.' King Stefan must have been exceptionally good, I thought, if he had such power to help others, despite having lain dead, stone dead, for hundreds of years.

Languages, religions and anti-religions have always mingled at the foot of Prokletije, so not only the Orthodox — the native Serbs and the Montenegrins — but everyone else believed in the healing and protective power of the holy king's bones and brought their children here to crawl through underneath them. Yes, Meliha and Trasha had done the same.

'It's a great sanctum. God protects the monastery from all troubles. There was never a fire. We Albanians protected it from the enemy when the Serbs had to leave. Didn't you know?'

***

Sometimes I dreamed of Stefan Dečanski, probably because I wondered why I alone of my whole generation had to get so seriously ill. Why was I singled out, isolated and incarcerated, why was I tormented by fear and troubling thoughts, night sweats and delirium? Why this punishment? What had I done to deserve this? I was a good student, a good child, a good friend. I was quiet.

In one dream, King Stefan, who was blinded by his father (and later killed by his own son!) but miraculously regained his sight, though he had to hide it because he knew it was better to be without eyes than without a head, rode toward me on a dappled grey horse. He smiled and wanted to explain something, but I was furious and spat blood and spewed fire at him. *I'm not Stefan, I'm Alyosha Karamazov*, he hurried to say. *You're not Alyosha*, I snarled and sent a burst of dragon fire at him that singed his hair, and then another. *You aren't, and even if you were, you're all the same. You didn't do anything for me — you were asleep when I crawled underneath the coffin, or you went off to act in some other play. Or you did it on purpose, to teach me a lesson. Why?! Maybe you even sent me your pain, the pain of a son and the even greater pain of a father. When my back brushed against the coffin you might not even have been in it. You betrayed me. I hate you!*

So I yelled in my sleep. I was angry, cried, spewed fire and spat blood again. And he, the king and saint, just sat there on his dappled grey and smiled from ear to ear.

THE BENCH BENEATH THE
MULBERRY TREE

Trasha's husband died long ago. She had four daughters and a whole gaggle of grandchildren. All her male children had died young.

In that respect, too, she resembled my grandmother Đurđa. Trasha liked me to tell her about her and my mother's village. Then she'd nod, as if her house also had an earthen floor in one part, where the wood stove was, and where straw was spread at Christmas. All the houses at that time were made of mudbricks and whitewashed. An Isabella grape vine sprawled over one wall. There was a mulberry tree at the front door with a bench beneath it, which offered a beautiful view of the large field of corn, the plum orchard and the vast plain in the distance. A small hill could be observed — bare, with dark, slab-like rocks. Enigmatic.

Grandmother Đurđa moved around on crutches. Back when World War II began, my mother's family fled to Montenegro. It was safer in Podgorica and they were able to make a living. The Allies bombed the city persistently towards the end of the war. Once a bomb landed in the River Morača, not far from where Đurđa and some other women were washing clothes. The explosion was so powerful that it flung them all into a recess in the riverbank and buried them up to their heads in sand and stones. People rushed to the scene and struggled to dig them out. From then on, my grandmother was in fragile health and increasingly less mobile. But she managed to do all the housework, with grandfather's help, and even milked several sheep.

She had great powers of endurance because she was so understanding. She always looked forward to visitors. When we came, she'd hurry as best she could on her crutches to bring me an egg freshly laid that morning, and to put more wood in the stove so the water would boil faster. She'd peel it while still hot — though freshly boiled eggs are hard to peel — salt it, and give it to me devotedly and contentedly, as if there had never been any wars, refugee treks and lice, as if there had never been hunger and children's coffins, and as if nothing had ever hurt, not even a little finger — as if nothing in the world was more important than a little girl getting a fresh, warm, salted egg from her grandmother's hand. Grandmother Đurđa's delight at giving me a treat shone like a second sun next to the one that nested up in the mulberry tree in front of the house and shed golden dust on us.

***

In 1928, the Kingdom of Yugoslavia granted land in Metohija to Montenegrins who came from rocky, waterless villages. Among them my grandfather, who received a five-hectare plot and built a small house by himself, being a skilled mason. It had two rooms and a hall, and it was made of adobe — unfired blocks of sun-dried mud.

The public land now settled by the Montenegrins had served the local Albanians as grazing land for centuries. It was known exactly who grazed their animals where, so care for the new settlers was divided up accordingly. When the Second World War began, the natives remained in the towns, while the new immigrants, uneasy and afraid of both the foreign occupiers and their neighbours, returned to their homeland. Their warm, white houses in Metohija, made of the earth watered and nourished by the goddesses of Prokletije, were soon ruins.

When the war ended, Grandfather Tomo came with Đurđa and their three girls... and saw that everything was gone. They slept in the open. The next morning, their rescuer appeared: Selman, an Albanian, and godfather of the children. There he was, with four sheep and an ox. And words of welcome. He helped them rebuild in the same place, this time a house of stone. Grandmother stewed nettles and made cheese from sheep's milk, while Grandfather Tomo joined together with our neighbour, Muamer, and with two oxen they ploughed others' land for a daily wage. In the autumn, he planted plum trees, and in the first spring after the war the state provided the farmers with seed, and they sowed corn and wheat. The Party kept things firmly under control, and progress began. And when everyone is doing well, and better, there's no enmity.

**

Grandfather Tomo was in the army when Axis forces invaded Yugoslavia in April 1941 and the country's defences collapsed.

He returned home mainly on foot under cover of the forests.

Pregnant, grandmother Đurđa left the cows, goats and the house and made it with her three girls to Peć, where Montenegrins were assembling to trek over Prokletije.

Two days passed and there was no sign of Tomo. The only news was bad news — about bombardments and the foreign occupation. Đurđa was increasingly worried and decided to go back for the cattle. She and another woman walked the almost thirty kilometres to Godfather Selman's house. That night, she gave birth to a son. In the morning, with Selman and his brother, she went to see the grim and unpredictable Uk Feta, who'd assembled all the abandoned cattle from several villages in his sheds. He was not exactly overjoyed to see her:

'Alright, Đurđa, you can have a look inside, but take someone else's cow and you're mincemeat!'

Đurđa hesitated. The threat was serious, and she was alone and unprotected, exhausted from childbirth. She could barely stand. She saw only deep darkness in the barn, full of cattle, sheep and goats. Then Selman came up to her and said, with his hand on his heart:

'You can go in. Don't worry. As long as there's a male child in my house no one will touch a hair on your head, or your family.'

Đurđa went into the darkness. The animals were crowded together and thirsty. Their breathing was laboured and they stirred.

She called her cows by name and they responded. Their mooing meant that she easily found them and led them out.

She stayed at Selman's for another two days. All the women and girls in the house prepared nappies, clothes and everything else needed for the baby, and then they put her on a horse and saw her to the city. Tomo arrived there too. But before the trek could leave, their little son died.

Grandmother Đurđa never wanted to talk about those times. I learned most of it from Trasha. It turned out that Selman was her paternal uncle, and the story about a Montenegrin woman who gave birth in his house became part of the family's oral tradition.

Narrow Street

Meliha's husband owned a jewellery shop in Narrow Street.

The street probably had another, more seemly name, but no one knew it.

Both narrow and short, it was the most exciting street in the city for girls and young women. Textile boutiques, goldsmith's shops, before whose windows the jewellery for the bride was agreed, variety stores, and a mosque at the beginning and end of the street, whichever your direction, and from where one turned and entered an even older trading area with butcher's shops and artisan's workshops — its allure was manifold.

Narrow Street was a paradise of shop windows with colourful sweets, foretokens, novelties and hidden treasure, rummaging through trinkets, searching and discovering, temptations and desires. At the same time, a parallel, invisible urban world dwelled here. Centuries old. I sensed it in the smell that lingered at the door of a goldsmith's shop, whose dusty display had no gold but only tarnished silver, always the same kind of filigree bracelets and clunky rings; or in the rustle when a woman in pantaloons went by; or in the breeze from Rugova Gorge that scampered over the roofs.

Peć is a city with an ancient history. There was much about

it we didn't know. But we were proud to live in the land of the Kosovo Myth, in the city that was the Serbian spiritual centre, the seat of the patriarchate, a city named after the hermit cells in caves at the entrance to Rugova Gorge. Even in prehistoric times, the caves served people as shelter from the elements in the Accursed Mountains; it was dry and they could light a fire on a stone floor.

In the golden fourteenth century, Peć was home to merchants, blacksmiths, tailors, masons, painters and filigree craftsmen. The nobility loved beautiful things that came from both east and west: elegant clothes, fine jewellery, handsome churches with stone ornamentation and magnificent frescoes. Peć is a beautiful city in a picturesque location, where the River Bistrica breaks free of the mountains' embrace and flows on, more tranquilly now, through the fertile land of Metohija to meet the White Drim. There was no lack of silver and silk, wine and saffron in those days.

***

It seems we're light years away from Narrow Street. Even further at night. Everything we push aside during the day emerges at night, swamps us like a giant wave and carries us away from the shore.

Fortunately, the Hospital for Pulmonary Diseases was surrounded by tall trees and the air was pleasant. Prokletije had its hand in healing and calming us.

***

Meliha was holding the cup even though she'd finished her coffee some while ago. Trasha, although still dressed, was curled up like a cat with a paw under its head, probably dozing, so I told Meliha, I guess to comfort her, that we'd be leaving Kosovo too.

Shortly before I'd coughed up blood the first time without warning, my family had bought a piece of land and started building a house. We didn't have enough money for the task, but my father sensed the direction in which things were developing and knew we'd have to leave sooner or later. Instead of going to Belgrade, where he was offered a fantastic job and an apartment, or to central France, where it seems there was demand for fruit growers, we, like our ancestors, followed our relatives to Montenegro, by the same route they always travelled — over the Čakor Pass.

The family kept me informed about every step: about the loan, about buying the windows and doors, and so on. And I was interested, but it seemed building the house would take a long time, years, and I didn't want to think about moving at all. There were so many more important things to me. In particular, I had to try and overcome my strange dreams. Every night, fear took on new forms.

Without Meliha and Trasha, I don't know if I'd have been able to haul myself out of that quicksand.

'Tuberculosis isn't really a pulmonary disease. Lungs don't hurt. It's your soul that hurts. You'll understand that better if you read *The Magic Mountain*. But not now. One day,' said the doctor — also a Sonja — seeing the blue volume of *The Idiot* on my bed.

FROM MY DIARY

Now that I've been here for four days, I wonder where my strength comes from to readily accept the fact that I have tuberculosis and will have to stay in hospital for at least three months.

I really try to use every moment. It's not what I'd prefer, but for now the time can be spent embroidering, reading magazines and studying.

Sometimes, when I go to bed, I wonder if I'm going to get deranged and stay that way. I mustn't think so much. My morbid imagination could just make my condition worse.

The room is small, clean and bright. The walls are painted pale green, the door is half-glazed and there are iron beds. I often look at the roses and chrysanthemums in the jar. The flowers make it so much more cheerful. I try not to feel like I'm ill.

***

Tuberculostatics — what a scary word. It makes me shake as if in a fever. There's nothing I can do. Streptomycin makes my face go numb, especially my chin and lips.

I mustn't be afraid, I mustn't.
I dream every night, and they're always weird dreams.
I cried for the first time in my six days here.
My chin is still shaking.
All my dreams are filled with fear.
Things take on a different form in the dark, in the silence, and a barking dog and the occasional bang of a door fill my bones with dread.

***

Today was such a wonderful day. First a letter came from Dragana. How wonderfully she can express feelings, give support and be a friend, both through words and with her beautiful handwriting, taking care to be legible and clear. She went to the trouble of copying and sending me Rudyard Kipling's wonderful poem 'If'. Then my whole class came to see me at the gate. Everyone! I was overjoyed to wave and be looking into those dear faces again: Rade, Zoran, Suzana, Ljubinka… I laughed and laughed until my jaws ached. It was wonderful!

It is worth living for them — for cheerful, good people and their happiness.

***

My face is disfigured with blotches and tiny pimples that itch. Sometimes I get the crazy desire to make a tapestry. To do as much as I can, as fast as I can. I'm too irritated to study. Everyone grates on my nerves — all those goggle-eyed old women, inquisitive girls and chatterboxes. To hell with them, I want to yell and scream, but nothing comes out. I just embroider and read in silence.

In the dining room, after dinner, I listened to the tambourines and watched the other patients dance.

***

The bells are ringing at the Patriarchal Monastery. The roses and chrysanthemums in the jar have begun to wither.

The family didn't come to visit last night. I sat alone on a green-painted bench in the park. It was dark and cold, but I kept waiting. There was a soft crackle down by my slippers in the fallen leaves, the branches of the nearby bush swayed slightly, and a bird flew off just over my head.

I've always relied on others. I've always been looking for someone, Mr Right, just for me. Can't I live by myself? Can't I give myself the comfort and strength I need to endure? Haven't I helped myself so many times, while hoping for a person with understanding who could do something for me?

***

I now belong to this hospital; this is my place; the order and harmony of the movements and procedures suits me perfectly.

The nurses in the hospital are quiet and very attentive. They do their best to cheer us up and look after us, especially us younger patients.

Last night I went for another walk in the park. I love the smell of rain-soaked earth, and whenever the pigeons, frightened by my presence, darted off from the branches, the remaining drops would fall on my head. The darkness thickened beneath the trees, and only the fallen but pristine yellow leaves gave light. Absolute silence.

I look at the face in the mirror: big dark rings around my eyes, a pronounced mark on my right cheek, chapped lips and greasy long hair without colour or shine. Dead.

***

A thirteen-year-old Albanian girl is in the bed next to me. Mehrija, from Istok. She managed to tell me, in broken Serbian, that her mother had been killed by lightning two years earlier, and now her father had died, two and a half months ago. They were six children. She was the oldest, and she took care of them all with the help of an uncle; one of her brothers was here too now, in the paediatric ward. She goes to school here and gets straight A's. Later she wants to become a doctor, and surprisingly, she's very cheerful. But the nights are restless for her, too. She talks constantly in her sleep, often loudly and angrily, and at times she even yells.

Sometimes I say: 'When I get out.' Then I think: 'If I ever get out.' I mustn't be like that.

Those nights... first you can't sleep, then you dream all sorts of nonsense, and in the morning you wake up nervous and edgy from doors slamming, people coughing and the tap-tapping of shoes.

My dreams are full of leering faces and strange creatures covered in white sheets. Like last night.

First there was a bang and then a bright light. A shape in white appeared, terribly white, and baring its teeth. I turned and fled, struggling to push open hundreds of heavy doors, but I felt the leaden hand of that figure weigh down on my shoulder, and I couldn't get away. I woke up crying.

I tried to stay awake. I fell asleep all the same, but now, in the second episode of the dream, there was a solution for everything: I found out that the police had arrested a man all in white who'd been going around pretending to be an alien and frightening people. Some fool. I woke up calm and free of fear, just with a stomach ache.

***

Last night I had a dream without drama: there was a dead cat, a kerosene lamp in the deep darkness and a pile of boxes.

My eyes hurt. White Nights will have to wait. The tapestry too. Why do I embroider mostly the same images: a house, a mountain and fir trees? I always finish the house first.

***

Tonight the patients invited a guy called Dragoljub to the dining room. He was a bit under thirty, tall and handsome, and his dark eyes burned strangely as if he was constantly looking at candles. Dragoljub is deaf, but he can lip-read very well. The women had collected money for him and now brought it to the table; they joked around and teased him a bit, but in a sisterly sort of way and he didn't mind. He counted 25,000 dinars and then said sadly: 'I need eighty, eighty thousand, for a pair of hearing aids.'

Then he asked the women to play some music and dance. They produced a tambourine. The women love these spells of freedom in the evenings and could hardly wait — they often sing and dance in the dining room. It seemed absurd to me at first. Where did their spirit come from and how could they be so cheerful in hospital? But now I enjoy watching the tambourines, pantaloons and flushed cheeks. Pure joy. I understood Dragoljub. It's not so bad when you see movements. It may seem inane and meaningless without music, to see the open mouths, swaying bodies, blinking, clapping, and you don't hear the song and laughter. But Dragoljub actually heard it all, in his own way. And enjoyed it. The joy of living.

***

If I ever have children, I mustn't let there be a single moment of negligence in their upbringing, that is, in living with them. To live with children means to regard them without condescension, to not overdo anything, and to give them plenty of love — so much that they understand that the love of beauty is the root of happiness. People and birds are beautiful, music and the guardian stone at the spring too, the horse chestnut leaf and the page torn out of a diary, and Picasso's quirky picture and the sea underfoot in the picture, in verse; a bee is beautiful with the heavy yellow sachets of pollen on its legs when it crash-lands near the hive's entrance and staggers inside; it's beautiful when Dad lends the car to a neighbour, and most beautiful on Sundays when we all sit together by the river, eat sandwiches, play and laugh — hearty, unrestrained, lachrymose laughter.

***

From the top of the stairs I watch her leave: a beautiful young blonde with an umbrella, in a warm burgundy coat. Solemn, white-clad pines and other tall trees stand on either side of the path as if to protect her; and the snow is falling steadily, silently, finer than fine, as if bashful. The benches, too, are hidden beneath a thick white blanket. Everything becomes greyer, quieter, still, and soon darkness will fall. Now I can no longer see my best friend, not even her footprints.

***

Meliha didn't speak the night before last, she just held my hand and looked from those inscrutable depths of hers.

My mother came to visit. She walked to the hospital in her old boots on the icy paths. And she had a cold. She'd queued in front of the shop for hours to buy milk, but it didn't arrive, so she couldn't bring me any. So she brought a pink jumper she'd knitted for me as a surprise.

My anxiety that I might have infected her, that she could get seriously ill and would have to lie in the same room, culminated around midnight. All my efforts to evoke images of meadows, butterflies and mountain springs were in vain. I shook more and more, the whole iron bed was shaking, and fits of trembling swept over me in waves, clenching me like a vice, especially my knees and shoulders. No, no, I resisted, how lovely it is to lie and soak up the sun, to relax; it will stop, it's sure to stop soon. And I'm here alone, without anyone

273

near and dear, but it's better like this, so they don't have to watch. I can't die now. I've only just become a young woman. Life is so beautiful, and I'll be with the others again, in the classroom and on my birthday. Maybe I'm really going to die. As a philosopher said: 'Death does not concern us, because as long as we exist, death is not here. And once it does come, we no longer exist.'

You coward! The trembling stopped. Then started again. You coward! It stopped once more. Now I know, I've changed. People need to be loved, they need to be trusted and forgiven. I must never again waste hours and days in dissatisfaction, in dark, aimless speculation and hatred, as I did before. Never again. Life is so precious — the forest, the sun on your cheeks. The trembling passed. My eyelids grew heavy. The mist carries me.

***

Last night, around ten, it happened all over again. First, unrest in my body, not in my mind. Currents coursing through my legs. I tried to embroider but threw everything down again, and the threads were a tangle all over the bed. Pain in my left side and a doctor who says my heart is fine. One, two, three tranquillisers. Every visit seems to make me too restless. Maybe it would be better if no one came, if only Trasha sat on her bed in silence and Meliha made the only real Turkish coffee as if in a trance — for as long as it takes for the pain to subside or drown itself.

***

They let me go home for the first time for New Year's Eve, to welcome in 1981. I'd heard snippets of news about events in the country, but it didn't let them detract from my joy at being together with the family again. The one-room flat is quite adequate for the five of us, even when the occasional relative is passing through.

I love the building we live in. I think it's the most beautiful in town. It once housed an agricultural school, so it's square and thick-walled, with two entrances and a wide hallway, all on one level, and its seven flats have a strange layout. The surroundings are the loveliest thing: two large parks, and behind the building is a row of new outkitchens and then garages. Most of the trees there are horse chestnuts with wide canopies. When the chestnuts blossom and their tall flower-clusters begin to sway like dervishes' hats, the park is as lavish as a maharaja's palace. In front of the building stands a giant, lone plane tree. The centre of our world.

I talked with the neighbours and my friends from the window, from a distance, just in case, though I was no longer considered infectious. But it was still fine like that. Everything was lovely. Life is good and perfect, whatever it brings — life will always be a bright new day in which the neighbours chatter like birds about a million infinitely interesting details.

***

Tomorrow it will be three months. The first negative came. Just a bit longer and I can be discharged.

It's so lovely outside. The snow fell first from a torn sky, and now it drops from the branches of the black trees. And peace, that solemn peace that people can't disturb. The sky, that morose, tarnished-silver sky, descends ever lower from the mountains. It seems about to fall, but nothing happens. A tiny man in a black coat, who constantly drags one leg behind him, continues on his aimless, drunken path, and I watch as the mist swallows him up. Soon all traces of him are gone, too.

People pass by, their heads bent and their hands deep in their pockets. A young man and woman, one umbrella. They look very much in love, but he — perhaps because he's so enamoured — has forgotten that the umbrella is for two, so the poor girl now wears a cap of snow.

A boy walks as if his path has no end. Sometimes he stops to prod a pebble with his shoe. Then he looks round after passers-by as if just waiting for the chance to relieve them of their wallet or at least a few coins for a bus ticket.

Oh yes, and a certain young gentleman, a student, came from Belgrade on holiday. He said to say hello, they told me.

Why am I certain we'll never meet again, at least not in this life?

LEAVING

Dear Trasha had no notion of national or ethnic groups. No one was pigeonholed, and at most she'd say 'the Albanian people', 'your people' or 'the peoples of Yugoslavia'.

'This won't end well,' she muttered and shook her head. 'Now with Tito gone, everyone will pull in their own direction and we'll be torn apart like a rag.'

The morning Meliha was discharged, without much joy, and sad to be leaving her beautiful city, Aunty Trasha died.

In fact, when I woke up her bed was empty and the sheets had been changed. Meliha, too, her small suitcase in hand, stood there confused. How could we not have heard anything?

That evening, the others could see me from the hallway: a skinny body in pyjamas looking out of the big window into the darkness and dancing. But I didn't care. I danced to the music from the transistor radio, for tired Trasha, sad Meliha and frightened me. I danced for life that goes on, carrying everything in its path, along with the three of us, like three dandelion seeds, or three snowflakes.

***

The following year, nothing was the same any more. Hatred arose and flourished. Suddenly it was all about 'us' and 'them'. On one side the Albanians, on the other everyone else. Albanian shopkeepers would no longer speak Serbian. The Gorani[3] in their pastry shop were scared — they'd quickly bring the salver with our favourite cakes to the table, without a smile, and return behind the glass showcase, whispering.

We were sad, and that despondency lasted for months. We went to the lyceum tense, followed by the worried gazes of our mothers. We needed passes to enter the school. The teachers were especially cautious during the breaks and monitored the movements of the students in the schoolyard. We could hardly wait for the school year to end. There would be no school prom because it was too great a risk.

We hadn't finished the house in Montenegro yet, but we left nonetheless. Father resigned from the Communist Party. His warnings that it was wrong to exclude Albanians from positions of power were unwelcome. Pressures and threats intensified, from all sides.

It was August again. Hot and tense. We sold our beehives. We sent a load with the removal men. Finally we got in our trusty old Škoda after going through the flat and the garage a hundred times. We left the potplants and gave the neighbours part of our winter stores. We said goodbye to everyone quickly and quietly, as if we were felons on the run.

The Bistrica, as usual, was bright. We stopped after five kilometres, as usual, to drink from the spring. We drove up into the heart of Rugova Gorge slowly, without words. I was

---

3 A Slavic Muslim ethnic group (literally 'Highlanders') that primarily inhabits the triangle between Kosovo, Albania and North Macedonia.

an adult and freshly enrolled at university, and I'm ashamed to admit that I felt sick, so I closed my eyes and breathed deeply.

I see the row of lilacs, the well, the chamomile around it, and the vast orchard in bloom. That whiteness is a consolation for me. I shoulder it and bear it with me. It's here, in safety.

DEDALUS CELEBRATING WOMEN'S LITERATURE 2018 TO 2028

Dedalus began celebrating the centenary in 2018 of women getting the vote in the UK by a programme of women's fiction. In 1918, Parliament passed an act granting the vote to women over the age of thirty who were householders, the wives of householders, occupiers of property with an annual rent of £5, and graduates of British universities. About 8.4 million women gained the vote. It was a big step forward but It was not until the Equal Franchise Act of 1928 that women over twenty-one were able to vote and women finally achieved the same voting rights as men. This act increased the number of women eligible to vote to fifteen million. Dedalus' aim is to publish six titles each year, most of which will be translations from other European languages, for the next ten years as we commemorate this important milestone.

Titles published so far are:

The Prepper Room by Karen Duve
Take Six: Six Portuguese Women Writers edited by Margaret Jull Costa
Take Six : Six Spanish Women Writers edited by Simon Deefholts & Kathryn Phillips-Miles
Slav Sisters: The Dedalus Book of Russian Women's Literature edited by Natasha Perova
Baltic Belles: The Dedalus Book of Estonian Women's Literature edited by Elle-Mari Talivee

The Dedalus Book of Knitting: Blue Yarn by Karin Erlandsson
The Victor by Karin Erlandsson
My Father's House by Karmele Jaio
Eddo's Souls by Stella Gaitano

For more information contact Dedalus at info@dedalusbooks.com

**Take Six: Six Portuguese Women Writers edited by
Margaret Jull Costa**

'Few of Portugal's female novelists are to be found in English
translation, which is as artistically regrettable as it is culturally
telling. This collection of masterful short stories represents
a notable and important stab at setting the record straight.
Varied in style and subject, all the stories share a remarkable
verve and freshness. Among the half-dozen writers selected is
Agustina Bessa-Luís, who penned the 1954 classic A Sibila
and whose death last year at the age of 96 provoked a day
of official mourning in her adopted city of Porto. Aficionados
of feminist literature should also check out New Portuguese
Letters, whose erotic and irreverent subject matter saw it
banned by the Salazar dictatorship. A worldwide cause celebre
in its day, one of its three authors – Maria Velho da Costa –
passed away late last month.'

Oliver Balch in The Guardian

£9.99   ISBN 978 1 910213 69 8   252p   B. Format

Take Six : Six Spanish Women Writers edited by Simon Deefholts & Kathryn Phillips-Miles

'Part of a wider collection bringing previously untranslated short stories to English-speaking audiences, *Take Six*'s opening author proves to be the ideal spokeswoman for its cause. Emilia Pardo Bazán's impassioned tone and uncompromising plots lay bare the very misogyny that has prevented her voice from being widely heard before now. And, like any girl group worth their salt, the authors that follow each add something fresh and distinctive to the mix.

Alongside Bazán's vehemence sit Carmen de Burgos' lyricism, Carmen Laforet's wistfulness, Cristina Fernández Cubas' surrealism, Soledad Puértolas' angst and Patricia Erlés' biting wit. Arranged chronologically according to the year of the authors' births, the volume doubles as an unexpectedly wonderful time machine, whisking the reader through over a century of changing styles, concerns and attitudes as it seeks to uncover a region of Spain's literary landscape where few British readers have ventured before.'

Rachel Rees in *Buzz Magazine*

£9.99   ISBN 978 1 912868 76 6   266p   B. Format